A CHRISTMAS TRUCE

An utterly addictive, feel-good festive romance
to fall in love with this Christmas

EMMA BENNET

Joffe Books, London
www.joffebooks.com

First published in Great Britain in 2023

Cover art by The Brewster Project

ISBN: 978-1-83526-201-6

To my O, I love you a quite ridiculous amount, my hairy hero x

CHAPTER 1

Libby Spellman stood by the photocopier, willing the machine to explain why its digital display kept flashing E95 at her.

"What do you want?" she hissed at it desperately. The stupid thing had spewed out the first twenty-two pages of the report she needed to make seven copies of, no problem, but had then decided to stop. It had plenty of paper. It didn't seem to be running low on ink. Frankly, she was stumped and was getting irrationally cross.

Closing the lid of the printer firmly and giving it a moment to consider its actions, Libby leant back against the magnolia wall and ran her fingers through her short blonde hair. She closed her eyes to block out the fluorescent strip lighting and temporarily freed her already sore feet from her black court shoes — it wasn't even 10.30 a.m., but she longed for them to be ensconced in her trusty Vans.

What was she doing, wasting her time photocopying reports about temporary traffic lights? Thank goodness she was only temping for this company. Imagine being stuck in a job like this permanently. She gave a little shudder and focused on throwing a few positive thoughts out into the universe that a more interesting position would come along for her soon.

Libby stretched; her limbs felt all scrunched up from being hunched over the machine despite the yoga class she'd taken the evening before. She needed coffee. Maybe she'd pop down the corridor to the staff room and use the fancy pod machine in there — about the only decent thing she could think of about working where she was. Maybe the printer would decide to play ball by the time she was back.

Abandoning her post, she found her way to the staff room, only getting a little bit lost twice, which was a definite improvement from the day before. She grimaced at the gaudy plastic Christmas tree in the corner — it wasn't even mid-November! She supposed it was up early because they had to eke out any joy they could working here. Libby loved Christmas but there was something very depressing about that tree.

A box of doughnuts was open on the counter next to the coffee machine with a note attached inviting you to, *Help yourself!*

Libby did just that, and felt decidedly more cheerful as she made her way back to the photocopier armed with carbs and caffeine. This position was only for a month, and then it really would be nearly Christmas. Robert had promised to take at least a week off and had hinted that he had something very important to ask her.

Lost in daydreams of her boyfriend down on one knee in her parents' sitting room on Christmas morning, she initially didn't hear someone call out behind her.

"Lizzy!"

She continued along the corridor until she heard the call repeated. Turning, she found her supervisor, Simon Manning, standing by his office door, looking rather pointedly at her.

"Sorry," Libby said, wiping sugar from her mouth. "Are you . . . were you talking to me?"

"Of course, I'm talking to you!" came the reply. "I called your name twice! I told you to do that photocopying for me. I need it for my Zoom meeting to discuss the council's major new zebra crossing strategy. Why are you wandering around the corridors with coffee and doughnuts?"

Libby's blue eyes flashed, but she managed to hold her tongue. "The printer . . ." she began.

"There's always an excuse with you people," said Simon, shaking his balding head. "This would be why you're still just a temp at, what, thirty?"

"I'm twenty-six," muttered Libby.

"Really, Lizzy, you know 'attitude is a choice', as Seth Coleman says." He indicated a book on his desk. *110%. Unleash your full potential with world-renowned entrepreneur, Seth Coleman*, declared the front cover.

"My name is *Libby*."

"You know what?" continued Simon, seemingly not having heard her, "Take this." He handed Libby the book, forcing her to awkwardly move the remains of her doughnut into the same hand as her coffee, causing it to squish against the cup. "It'll change your life."

"Er, thanks . . ." said Libby.

"But don't you let me catch you reading it when you're supposed to be doing my photocopying!" Simon added. "Now, off you toddle."

Libby lacked the words to explain to Simon just how offensive he was, and so she reminded herself that she'd be out of this job the moment something else came up before she followed his advice, and toddled. She'd met plenty of managers like him before, and would no doubt meet many more. Dealing with them seemed to be part and parcel of working temp jobs.

She found the photocopier still refusing to cooperate. The only other trick she had up her sleeve was to switch it on and off at the wall. Libby swallowed the last bite of doughnut and placed the book Simon had given her on the printer. She reached up with her free hand to the power socket, the mug of coffee in her other hand, holding it as high out of the way as she could. She couldn't quite flick the switch and inched further, going up on her tiptoes. Just when she was stretched to her absolute limit, she once again heard, "Lizzy! Have you still not finished that photocopying? My meeting's in five minutes and the head of communications is waiting!"

Libby jumped, spilling her still full cup of coffee on and down the back of the printer.

Simon's exasperation exploded. "What the hell have you done?"

"I'm so sorry!" Libby gasped. "I'll clean it up straight away!"

But before she could even find something to begin mopping the liquid up, the lights went out with a pop.

"What's happened?" someone shouted out. "My computer just shut itself off, and I hadn't saved the file I was working on!"

"What's going on with the power?!" another voice yelled.

Simon's round face had turned redder than Libby had thought was possible.

I guess that's the end of another job then, thought Libby. She threw the coffee-soaked book Simon had given her into the bin on her way out.

* * *

And so it came to chance that by midday Libby was sitting on a chair in the offices of her friend Melissa's temp agency in the centre of Weybridge, with trainers on her relieved feet, and a replacement coffee in hand.

"So, what do you fancy next?" asked Melissa, turning to her computer screen and tying back her long, dark hair — always a sign she was going into serious business mode. She'd been dealing with Libby's frequently changing jobs for so long that finding something new no longer fazed her, and if not for Libby's numerous visits to the offices of the temp agency the pair of them might never have become such close friends.

"I don't know, something different . . ." said Libby, hopefully.

"I'm afraid there's not much that's different in the world of temping at the moment. I've got the usual bar work and office admin . . ."

Libby sighed inwardly. It wasn't Melissa's fault. It was all very well being a free spirit and not allowing herself to get tied to a permanent job, but she wished there was something more interesting on offer for her to do. And something that paid better. It was rubbish never having any spare cash and she was getting a little old for the broke student lifestyle. Of course, it would help if she didn't have such an expensive photography habit to fund — macro lenses didn't come cheap and there always seemed to be something she was desperate to buy for her hobby.

"There's a live-in position available," Melissa said. "Free accommodation and the pay is better than anything else I have to offer. It's based on St George's Hill and there's the possibility of international travel. It's advertised as a personal assistant placement, but you'd basically be a girl Friday to a businessman." She looked up at Libby and shrugged. "I don't think you'd be bored at least."

"That doesn't sound much like a temp job," commented Libby.

"No, it's definitely long-term. I think he tried a recruitment agency but didn't get on with the people they sent. He's too busy to interview a load of candidates in person himself, he said, so he asked me to recommend someone who, I quote, 'can use a computer and has more than two brain cells to rub together.' Naturally, I thought of you."

"Thanks!" said Libby, laughing. "He sounds an absolute delight, but I'm not sure Robert would be too impressed if I moved out to live with another man."

"I know, I know. I just think it would suit you. It would certainly be more interesting than filing old law reports."

Libby pulled a face: that particular job had been a definite low point.

"Well, call me if anything else comes up," Libby said.

"Of course, I will."

* * *

As Libby left the office, the heavens opened. Oh, how she often wished she was the type of person who carried an umbrella with her. She was perfectly organised and capable when it came to work – recent printer escapades aside, but Libby's aversion to planning did occasionally lead to situations like this.

She pulled her coat hood up, took her mobile out of her bag and tried calling Robert, thinking maybe he'd like to meet her for some lunch if he could get away from the office for a bit. Disappointingly, the call went straight to voicemail.

While debating what to do with the rest of her day, the bus home came into view. A sign! She hurried to the bus stop, doing her best to keep her shoes out of puddles, and hopped on when the bus pulled up.

It wasn't a long journey and soon Libby was outside her home and fishing around in her backpack for her keys.

The front door wasn't double-locked as Robert liked it to be — she must have forgotten to do it when she left earlier. Lucky she'd got home before him and escaped the inevitable lecture.

Sighing, Libby headed straight up to the main bedroom so she could get out of her work clothes and into something more comfortable. Then maybe she'd start a Netflix marathon while she trawled job sites. Again.

She opened the door to the bedroom to find Robert and a very bendy dark-haired woman in a rather compromising and extremely naked position on her bed.

Libby froze, so shocked she didn't know what to say or do.

In contrast, Robert frantically leapt up, red in the face, while the mystery woman yanked the duvet over herself. He grabbed his trousers from the floor and pulled them on, not meeting Libby's eyes.

Libby managed to find her voice. "I thought you were at work," she said, lamely.

"Lunch break . . ." muttered Robert, hunching his tall frame over as if to protect his modesty.

Libby turned and walked right back out of the house. If she'd been more observant when she'd arrived home, she'd have noticed Robert's car parked a little further down the road. She resisted the urge to drag her front door key down its side.

Libby marched along the grey, suburban pavements in no particular direction, trying to get her head around what had happened. The November drizzle didn't even register anymore.

She and Robert were certainly different, but they'd been rubbing along together for a long time. They'd built a life as a couple. If he wasn't happy, they could have talked about it, at least attempted to work things out. Surely they owed that to each other? A wave of anger washed over her. How could he cheat on her after all this time? And she'd thought he was going to propose at Christmas!

She walked in a daze, no destination in mind, trying to process what had happened and the ramifications of it. It wasn't long before practicalities forced themselves to the forefront of her mind: what was she supposed to do now? She had nothing with her other than what was in her bag, but she couldn't go back to the house to pick up anything else. Not while they could still be there.

She was too stunned to cry. She felt so stupid.

She'd been wandering aimlessly for at least half an hour when her mobile rang — it was Robert. *He took his time*, Libby thought wryly. Did he take the chance to finish off what he'd been doing before getting in touch? She didn't answer the call; she had no desire to speak to him. Nothing he had to say would change the situation she now found herself in.

The ringing of the phone stopped but resumed again almost immediately. He called a total of four times before leaving a voicemail message. Libby's curiosity got the better of her and she decided to listen so she could find out what exactly it was that Robert was so desperate to tell her.

"I suppose I can't blame you for not picking up. I'm going back to work now, I've got that meeting I told you about this afternoon . . . Obviously, we need to talk — I'm an idiot and she means nothing. I'm sorry. You have to know this will ever happen again—"

It was at that point Libby abruptly deleted the message — she'd heard as much as she needed to: Robert wasn't home. Increasing her pace, Libby used a far shorter route to return to the house she and Robert had shared for the last two years, her mind racing, planning what she needed to pack. She didn't own much that was worth anything — she'd never had the finances to buy expensive things, and any extra money she did have, she chose to save for travelling, for adventures Robert had increasingly become too busy at work to go on — but she did have books, photographs and mementoes that she wouldn't want to abandon. She couldn't take all that now though. She'd have to pack the essentials and come back for the rest another time.

Libby knew her mum and dad would happily have her stay with them for as long as she needed, but going back to her childhood bedroom with her tail between her legs would, she suspected, only make her feel even more sorry for herself. Plus, being in the little village she grew up in wouldn't exactly be conducive to her finding work which interested her and paid a decent wage. No, she'd be better off staying in Weybridge and accepting the job Melissa had talked about earlier. She gritted her teeth and called her friend.

Melissa answered the phone after two rings. "Surrey Temps."

"Hi, Melissa, it's Libby."

"Hiya, Lib! What can I do for you?"

"I got home to discover Robert's been cheating on me," Libby said, tears threatening at the corners of her eyes.

There was a sharp inhale of breath at the end of the phone. "Oh no! Are you sure?"

"I caught him in our bed with another woman. I'm sure."

"I'm so sorry, sweetie. What an idiot!"

"He's certainly that," said Libby, her ire helping her to hold her tears in check. "Anyway, I think I'll have to apply for the job we talked about earlier if it hasn't gone already . . ."

Libby crossed her fingers. The job required someone to start straight away and included accommodation, so would solve her housing problem. She only hoped it hadn't been snapped up by somebody else, especially as the pay was much better than anything else going.

"It's still available," Melissa said, her voice sympathetic. "But I should warn you, the guy you'd be working for is apparently a bit particular about who he has on his staff."

"I'm desperate," said Libby bluntly before adding, "How particular are we talking?"

"To be honest, I'm not sure. As it's a live-in position it may be that he's just quite fussy about who he has staying in his home. You'll have to sign a confidentiality agreement."

"Seriously?"

"I'm afraid so."

"Alright," Libby agreed reluctantly. What else could she do?

"Brilliant. You'll need to do a telephone interview with him, but if he likes you, the job's yours."

"How soon could I do the interview?"

"I'm not sure," said Melissa. "Let me give him a call and I'll get back to you in a few minutes."

Libby reached the house, and let herself in. Robert had remembered to double lock the door this time. Despite her heartbreak, she found herself rolling her eyes. Going straight up to the bedroom, being very careful to avoid looking at the bed, she took her suitcase down from the top of the wardrobe and began methodically packing her clothes.

At the thought of the fallout from Robert's actions, as well as the fact she was currently jobless, without even realising she was doing it at first, Libby began to cry. She felt so hurt and betrayed.

After a moment, she wiped her tears away crossly. There would be plenty of time for self pity later, but, right now, she needed to get her stuff out of this house.

As Libby was trying to decide how many pairs of jeans she actually needed, her phone rang again. Assuming it was

Melissa ringing back, she answered it absentmindedly and without checking who the caller was.

"Hiya," she said.

"Good afternoon, am I speaking with Ms Spellman?" replied a deep, male voice.

"Yes," said Libby, cautiously.

"This is Seth Coleman. I believe you requested an interview for the position of my personal assistant?"

"Seth Coleman? *The* Seth Coleman?" Libby asked, recalling the book cover on her ex-boss's desk. *Was that really only a few hours ago?*

"I'm guessing so."

"The entrepreneur, Seth Coleman?" she clarified.

"Yes," said Seth, beginning to sound impatient. "If it's convenient, I have a few questions I want to ask you."

"Um, yeah, sure."

"Right, so firstly, if women and men lived on two different planets what would life be like on both of these planets?"

"Seriously?" Libby asked, incredulously.

"Yes, seriously."

Libby sighed; she could do without this rubbish right now. If she didn't really need this job, she'd be tempted to put the phone down and forget all about it. But the fact was, she wasn't in a position to do that. "Well, neither would last very long without any way to reproduce, so by the time we heard about these planets, the humans on them would be extinct."

"I meant for you to comment on the differences between the planets."

Libby was silent.

"Okay, moving on," said Seth. "Would you open an envelope that has the date of your death inside?"

"Who gave it to me?"

"Sorry?"

"Who gave me the envelope? Where did they get it? Do they know when I'm going to die? Are they planning to kill me?"

A pause. "I don't know . . ." Seth replied. He sounded thoughtful. "If you were a fruit, which would you be and why?"

"Look, Mr Coleman. I'm organised, I can type and I'm not afraid of hard work. If I have to answer what fruit that would make me . . . let's go with an apple, shall we?"

"Would you be able to start immediately?" he asked.

"As soon as you'd like me to," said Libby.

"Thank you for your time, Ms Spellman, I'll be in touch," Seth concluded before ending the call.

Libby put down her mobile in a daze. That was without doubt the strangest job interview she'd ever done. She suspected she'd mucked it up soundly, but frankly, she'd worry about that later.

Libby returned to her packing, but it wasn't long before her phone rang again. She checked it before answering this time and was relieved to see Melissa's number flashing up on the screen.

"It seems he likes you," Melissa said. "He's offered you the job!"

"Oh, that's great," said Libby, with a sigh of relief. *How on earth had that crazy conversation resulted in her being offered employment?*

"You can start tomorrow morning. If you pop back into the office now, I'll print out your contract and the confidentiality agreement for you to sign."

"Thank you so much, Mel. Why don't I grab us a couple of coffees on the way?" Libby suggested.

"Great! Make mine a latte."

"No problem. I'll see you soon."

Libby arrived back at Melissa's office laden with drinks and an enormous suitcase as well as her backpack and a bag containing her camera equipment. She handed a latte to her friend who accepted it gratefully.

"This would certainly be a good way to butter me up before you ask if you can crash at my flat tonight," Melissa commented as she took a sip.

Libby grinned. "Is this the right time to ask if I can crash at your flat tonight?"

"It's the perfect time, and, of course, you can stay, as long as you don't mind kipping on the sofa," Melissa said, giving her a sympathetic look.

"The sofa's fine, and thank you," replied Libby, hugging her friend. "I really appreciate it. I'll treat us to whatever takeaway you fancy."

"No, you won't," said Melissa firmly. "I'll cook. You pick us up a cheap bottle of wine if you like, but you're not forking out for a takeaway."

"You're the best!"

"I know!" retorted Melissa with a smile. "Now, let's get this contract signed."

CHAPTER 2

When she woke up on a strange sofa the next morning it took Libby a moment to work out where she was and why her stomach was in turmoil with stress and nerves. Then it all came flooding back: her boyfriend was cheating on her — in their own bed, no less — she had no home, and she was starting a brand-new job with an employer who appeared to be at least mildly deranged. It wasn't really surprising she felt nervous.

After they'd eaten the delicious risotto Melissa had made for supper the night before, Libby had decided to google her new boss, Seth Coleman. She thought she'd heard the name even before she'd seen it on the book cover, and as soon as she typed his name into the search engine, she remembered why. He was a renowned property developing entrepreneur, public speaker and author — his book had sold more than three million copies. He'd done a TED talk, for goodness' sake.

"Morning, lovely," said Melissa cheerfully appearing at the living room door. "I made you tea."

"Thank you," Libby said, taking the drink gratefully.

"How are you doing?"

Libby forced a smile onto her lips. "Not too bad," she said. "And today's got to be better than yesterday, right?"

"Absolutely," replied her friend. "Would you like a lift to work?"

"That would be great, as long as you're sure it won't make you late though?"

"Nah, it's not far out of my way. Will you be ready to leave by 8.20?"

"Sure, is it all right for me to have a shower?"

"Course. There should be plenty of hot water. Clean towels are in the linen cupboard outside the bathroom."

Libby showered, ate a couple of slices of toast with peanut butter and put on her smartest work clothes — she wasn't sure what the dress code would be, but decided it would be better to be overdressed for her first day than underdressed.

* * *

Libby had never been on St George's Hill before, but she'd heard a little about it since moving to Weybridge five years before. Back then, she'd had a nice flat and had just met Robert, plus Weybridge was a quick train journey into London to see old uni friends and get a hit of culture whenever she felt like it. She saw no reason to leave the area when she left the job she'd moved there for, and so she'd joined Melissa's temp agency, ensuring a fairly steady stream of income from jobs which didn't take over her life and left her free to go travelling whenever she liked.

All she knew about the Hill was that it had a golf club and a tennis club, and the houses cost an absolute fortune.

They followed the sat nav's directions which led them to one of the Hill's private entrances. A large security guard sat in a wooden hut by the side of the road.

"Where are you visiting?" the guard asked.

"Whitehaven!" called back Melissa. "Just dropping off Mr Coleman's new PA."

The security guard gave a nod in confirmation, and the barrier lifted.

They drove along the tree-lined road into the depths of St George's Hill, Libby sneaking a peek at as many of the amazing houses as she could, despite a lot of them being behind high stone walls.

They turned down a side lane and saw the sign for Whitehaven, her new home and place of work.

"Oh my goodness," gulped Libby, gazing up at the eight-feet-high black wrought-iron gates ahead.

Melissa leant out of her open car window, pressed the buzzer and a moment later, the gates began to open.

"Thank you for the lift," Libby said, trying to disguise the nerves in her voice. "I'll be fine on my own from here."

Melissa frowned. "Are you sure?"

"Yeah, don't be late for work. I'll message you later," Libby promised. She couldn't explain why, but it was important to her to go in by herself, to prove she could step into her new life.

"Okay, but I'm at the end of the phone if you need me," Melissa said.

"I know, thanks."

Libby climbed out of the car and waved goodbye before turning back to face the open gates. Walking through them, she continued slowly up the gravel driveway to the large, modern, stark white building ahead of her. The nearby matching garage was bigger than the house she'd shared with Robert.

Libby rang the doorbell and it was answered by a small, dark-haired woman wearing a navy blue apron over jeans and a t-shirt.

"You must be Seth's new PA," the woman said, smiling welcomingly.

"Yes, hi. I'm Libby."

"And I'm Sarah, Seth's cook and housekeeper. Come on in."

"Thanks," Libby replied, pulling her wheelie suitcase behind her.

15

The entrance hall was double height and flooded with light from the huge windows surrounding the door and a lightwell at the top of it. The staircase took centre stage and wound up to a balconied landing. Sarah led Libby through to the kitchen which was enormous, taking up most of the back of the house.

"Let me quickly finish kneading this bread dough, and then I'll show you around," Sarah offered.

She gave the dough a last few pummels before putting it in a bowl covered with cling film.

"Seth's locked himself in his office for the day, but he's left instructions for you in your office," Sarah explained. "I don't know how much you've been told about what you'll be doing. Knowing Seth, not much, but his secretary deals with the property business side of things. You're more in charge of the personal stuff — booking flights and hotels, helping with his blog and research for his books, and organising his charitable donations. Have you heard of the Coleman Trust?"

Libby shook her head.

"It's a trust Seth set up to help young people locally. It's been going for a few years now."

"Cool," said Libby. She liked the idea of getting involved in the charitable side of Seth's work.

Everything in the house was shiny and modern, and Libby was terrified she'd leave footprints all over the sparkling clean floors as Sarah led her to her new room.

"So Seth's suite is upstairs, then there are three other ensuite bedrooms up there. Your living space is here on the ground floor. It actually leads off from your office."

They went into a large, bright office, with a MacBook, iPad and iPhone neatly on the desk. "Those are for you," Sarah said. "The chair's ergonomic, but order yourself a standing desk if you'd prefer."

Sarah opened another door and stepped aside to allow Libby through. Any worries she might have been harbouring about whether she'd have enough room for all her stuff were immediately assuaged: her space was huge — a self-contained flat. She had her own bedroom, bathroom, and sitting room.

There was even a little tea and coffee making area with a mini fridge as if she was living in a hotel.

Like everything in the house, it was predominantly white and made Libby feel untidy. Her head began planning how she could soften it up a little — a colourful throw on the bed would help, maybe some cushions and a table lamp or two to use instead of the bright ceiling spotlights.

She was brought back to earth again by Sarah asking if she'd like a tour of the rest of the house.

Libby was shown room after beautiful room. The place was amazing, but she began to worry that her naturally messy ways might not gel too well with someone who chose to live in such a minimalist haven. Libby loved colour and to be surrounded by books, knick-knacks, and photos of her family and friends and places she'd visited. Walking through this house made her feel like she was in an Ikea showroom.

They went out of the glass doors in the kitchen and onto the terrace and found themselves facing an extremely handsome young man, wearing a tight t-shirt and shorts, digging in one of the flower beds with a spade. He was tanned and muscular with shoulder-length blond hair.

"Blimey. I suppose there are some benefits to global warming," Libby muttered.

"Jamie!" Sarah called out. "Put your jumper back on; it's freezing and there are women around!"

Jamie turned and caught Libby's gaze. She felt her cheeks redden immediately.

"Pardon, ladies, do forgive me," he said, grinning and giving an exaggerated bow. He picked up a black hoodie which lay to the side of him and put it on.

"Libby here is Seth's new PA," Sarah said. "Jamie's our gardener and general Mr Fix-It."

"Nice to meet you, Libby," Jamie said, giving her another smile.

An alarm rang out from Sarah's phone. "That's my cue to check on the bread," she said. "Jamie, have you got a few minutes to show Libby around the gardens?"

"Sure," Jamie replied. He wiped his hands on his trousers to get rid of some of the soil.

"Come back to the kitchen when you're done and I'll get the coffee machine on," Sarah called as she hurried inside.

Going round the side of the house, they came to another building. "The swimming pool's in there," Jamie pointed out.

"He has his own *swimming pool*?"

"Yep," Jamie replied casually. "Seth wanted an outdoor one, but I convinced him he'd only be able to use it a few times a year. The gym's in there as well."

The garden wrapped around the whole house and included a wooded area and an ornamental pond as well as the terrace. Flanked by heaters was a large table and chairs for entertaining, beside a covered area with a pizza oven and the largest grill Libby had ever seen.

Trying not to seem too intimidated, Libby turned to Jamie. "So, what's it like working for Seth?"

Jamie shrugged, considering. "It's good," he said. "He's not around much so I kind of just get on with things. He's quite particular with what he wants, but that's cool."

"Have you worked for him long?"

"A couple of years. I started off doing odd jobs, but now I'm full-time."

Jamie returned to work and Libby went back inside to find Sarah, who made her a coffee. "Would you like me to show you how to use the coffee machine?" Sarah asked, handing her a drink.

"I think I'll just stick to instant if I'm by myself. Just the sight of that thing terrifies me," admitted Libby.

Sarah smiled. "Fair enough, it is pretty intense. Seth takes his coffee seriously."

"I'll try to remember not to offer him a cup of my Nescafé then!"

They both laughed.

"Right, so, details of your work email address and log in details are on your desk," Sarah explained. "Seth should have emailed you about what he'd like you to do while he's away and what his itinerary is. He also said to tell you to take today to get acclimatised."

"Thanks," said Libby, turning to head towards her office. "I'll see you later."

"Oh," said Sarah, "And don't worry about dressing so smartly." She quickly added, "Unless you want to, of course. You look lovely. It's just Seth doesn't expect it."

Libby felt a wave of relief. "Thanks for the heads-up.".

"Would you like lunch at one? I can bring it through to you."

"You don't need to make me lunch!"

"It's in my job description, and it'll only be a sandwich — it's no big deal." said Sarah easily. "I'll be having mine at the same time, so we can take a lunch break together if you want?"

"Sounds good. See you at one then," said Libby, still not a hundred percent happy about having Sarah run around making food for her.

Libby went into her pristine office and opened the folder next to her new gadgets. In it, she found a copy of her new boss's itinerary as well as a list of everything she'd be expected to do on a day-to-day basis. She was excited to see the section about accompanying Seth on international business trips. That was a very definite perk of the job!

She spotted another folder in the top drawer of her desk labelled 'Household' which contained details of all the passwords she'd need to access everything she'd use for work as well as details about the house, including where spare keys were kept and the code to get into the garage.

She gratefully changed into jeans and one of her favourite tops, and spent the time until lunch setting up her new laptop and phone, and then couldn't resist googling how much they were worth. The result was quite astounding, especially for someone who always bought her tech second-hand and never had the latest models.

At one p.m., Libby went back into the kitchen to find Sarah serving up roast chicken salad sandwiches made using the just-baked bread.

"Thanks, this looks delicious," Libby said, sitting on a stool at the island. She still felt a little strange about having her lunch prepared for her by someone she didn't really know and also who she wasn't paying.

Sarah sat down next to her. "I'm starving," she confessed. "I don't know how I've managed to resist that bread while it's been cooling for the last hour."

As they enjoyed their lunch together, Libby found herself beginning to relax — she liked Sarah and Jamie, and the house, especially her space in it, was more than she could have imagined.

* * *

Jamie left at three, and Sarah soon after so she could pick her teenage son up from his school and take him for a dentist appointment. Libby continued fiddling around with her new tech and reading up on the notes Seth had left her until five. The job seemed pretty straightforward — most of it involved keeping track of Seth's diary, reminding him of appointments, booking appointments, and, it seemed, making sure that as few people as possible interrupted him at all times. The hours could be a little up in the air, especially if they were travelling or she needed to accompany him to an event, but that was fine. She didn't mind being accommodating. It wasn't like she had a boyfriend to get home for anymore. It didn't seem like it would be the most exciting work, but it was well paid and the opportunity to hopefully do some travelling was a good unexpected bonus. And she was looking forward to finding out more about the charity side of Seth's businesses. All in all, it seemed like the perfect job to see her through this rubbish chapter of her life and would give her the time and space to work out what she wanted to do long term without having to worry about finding a place to live.

Libby's good mood began to rapidly diminish, however, as evening drew in. It was more than a little creepy to be alone in a huge unfamiliar house. She guessed that Seth was around, but she couldn't be sure. It didn't help that the walls around the grounds were so high that you couldn't see any other houses, even if you wanted to.

As it was her first night, Sarah had left butternut squash lasagne for Libby's supper, with a post-it note stuck on top giving instructions on how to heat it up.

While it was warming, she pondered. Was she supposed to take her food through to her flat and eat there and then bring the plate back out to the kitchen? As she was by herself, she usually would have taken her food through to the sitting room, and eaten it in front of the television for company, but she didn't feel comfortable doing that here — what if she dropped food on the sofa? And setting the huge dining room table for just herself was ridiculous. As the timer pinged she settled on perching with her, admittedly delicious, supper at the end of the kitchen island.

It was so strange to have had her entire life turned upside down in less than two days. When she'd woken up the morning before, she had a different home and a job, not to mention a boyfriend, and she'd been so looking forward to Christmas. And now, here she was, single and sitting in this beautiful house she now lived in, and with a new job which sounded like it was going to be a lot more interesting than her last few. It seemed she'd truly landed on her feet. In that respect, at least.

Scooping up another fork of the delicious pasta, she couldn't help thinking that she wouldn't be in this situation if Robert hadn't cheated on her. Or at least if she hadn't caught him cheating, she thought cynically. He could have been sleeping with that woman for months for all Libby knew, she contemplated calmly. What if she hadn't spilt her coffee over the photocopier and left that awful job? She might still be in the dark about what Robert was really like.

Of course she was terribly hurt by what Robert had done — she'd thought they were going to spend the rest of their lives together. It was inexcusable, and she'd never forgive him, but she was grateful she was out of a relationship which obviously wasn't as solid as she'd thought it was, and that she was managing to move on from it . . .

She was also a little surprised she wasn't more upset about the fact that she and Robert were no longer together, and that the future she'd anticipated wouldn't be hers. Thinking about it now, she'd always known theirs wasn't a great romance. They'd begun dating, liked each other, and continued up the traditional relationship rungs. Each step was so gradual and expected, that Libby wondered whether she'd ever actually taken the time to consider whether she should even be with Robert at all.

Determining not to be maudlin, Libby propped her new phone up against the enormous vase of lilies in the centre of the island and played some music on Spotify to break the silence of the room — she didn't dare try the house's music system just yet. According to Sarah, it could be programmed to play music wherever you wanted in the house, including the bathrooms and the terrace. But as soon as Libby had set eyes on the controls, she'd envisaged nineties techno music blaring into every room at 3 a.m. because she'd pressed something she shouldn't — no, it was far simpler to steer clear.

She stood up to scrape the remains of food from her plate into the food recycling bin and, as she did so, glimpsed something moving on the other side of the glass doors. She froze. As she looked closer, and two eyes gleamed out of the darkness. A fox stood staring at her in the gloom.

Libby smiled with relief. "Good evening, Mr Fox," she said. She moved slowly closer, but the animal's bravery deserted him, and he ran away, disappearing into the darkness.

She went back to her clearing up with a smile — she'd come face to face with a fox for the first time in her life, she had a great new job and an amazing new home. This felt like a whole new start for her, and even if she did still feel a little bit like crying, Libby was determined to make the most of it.

CHAPTER 3

When Libby went into the kitchen the next morning, Sarah was already there.

"Would you like me to make you something for breakfast? I usually cook Seth an egg-white omelette, or there's homemade granola in the cupboard. Or would you rather sort yourself out?"

"I'll just make myself some toast, if that's alright?"

"Of course." Sarah smiled. "Let me get you a coffee though."

"That would be lovely, thank you," said Libby, gratefully. There was still no sign of her boss. Presumably, he'd have to show himself some time. He did live here, after all!

When Libby logged into her new email after breakfast, she discovered a message from Seth outlining what he'd like her to do for the day. It all seemed pretty straightforward, and the last item on the list was of particular interest to Libby — Seth needed some photos taken of the inside of his house for his social media accounts and blog. One of Libby's main duties was to run these accounts — a slightly intimidating task, as they all had well over a million followers — but the idea of spending her day being paid to take photos definitely appealed. Was she ever going to meet her elusive boss though?

Libby quickly worked through her other tasks and popped back into the kitchen to check in with Sarah and get some lunch. Jamie was also taking a break, chatting with Sarah and enjoying a cup of tea while Sarah cleaned the oven. Libby joined them, helping herself to a salad with some of Sarah's homemade quiche.

As soon as Libby finished eating, she went back to her office and eagerly grabbed her camera equipment. It was a beautiful, bright day, so she had all the natural light she needed, which was just as well because she'd never been able to afford lamps for her photography. She'd never been able to afford any new camera equipment actually — it was all second-hand.

Granted, furniture wasn't the most exciting subject to be photographing, but it was fun to set up the shots for the best angles and rearrange things a little to get the 'look' she felt Seth was going for, judging by his other social media posts — clean lines, functional and minimal — with a few carefully positioned books on stoicism or pieces of artwork from his travels. The photos would serve a variety of purposes, but were mainly to accompany blog posts detailing the perfectly curated life he led.

She wondered how long she'd need to live in this house until it began to feel like home to her. Or would she end up leaving before that happened? Then again, she wondered whether anyone could ever feel really comfortable here — the building's stark, white austerity didn't exactly scream cosy sanctuary to her, and Seth didn't appear to have put a lot of effort into personalising the space.

She took photos until she was losing the natural light, and then plugged her camera's SD card into her MacBook and began choosing her favourites of the hundreds of images. She was pleased when the photos were displayed on the larger screen; they were sharp and well set up — she thought they'd look great on Seth's blog.

Checking the time, Libby was amazed at how late it was — the afternoon had whizzed by. The only break she'd taken since lunch was when Sarah came to bring her a cup of tea and to say she was heading home.

The tea had gone largely undrunk and now Libby realised how thirsty she was. She fetched herself a big glass of water. It was also past time for her to clock off for the day. She attached the best pictures to an email and sent it to Seth before turning off her computer.

The thought of the long evening stretching ahead of her was not overly appealing, but without a car, there wasn't a lot she could do. She didn't feel comfortable inviting anyone over and a taxi into town would be expensive.

Just as she was beginning to feel lonely, her phone dinged and she was pleased to see a WhatsApp message from Melissa, checking up on her and wondering if she was free to meet up at the weekend.

All good here, thanks! No sign of the man himself yet. Dinner on Sunday? Libby replied.

Definitely, Melissa texted back.

There were a variety of healthy, individual meals cooked and stored in the freezer, each carefully labelled with their nutritional content. She'd been told to help herself, but Libby fancied a treat to celebrate her new start — a treat consisting of enough carbs to fuel a cyclist on the Tour de France. So she ordered herself a large pizza with extra cheese, a bottle of Diet Coke, and a tub of Ben and Jerry's to be delivered.

While she waited she found the password for Seth's Netflix account which was under 'Entertainment' in the house folder.

An hour later, Libby was in her PJs, groaning on the sofa after consuming all of the pizza. Congratulating herself on her restraint that she at least managed to leave half of the ice cream for another night, she settled down to a Netflix marathon.

* * *

The following morning, Libby logged on, keen for Seth's feedback on the photos. Her heart sank a little when she found no reply to her email. She'd been proud of her photographs and felt they deserved some recognition. She gave herself a mental shake. Maybe she was being silly. After all, they were just some photographs of Seth's house, which he was paying her to take — should she really expect thanks from him? But then it wasn't really thanks she was after, more a confirmation that they were what he'd wanted, and that she'd done a good job.

Not that there were no emails from Seth. He wrote all his own social media and blog posts, many about his life as an entrepreneur and he'd sent her some new content to put up online – a post extolling the virtues of a high-protein, low-carb breakfast. Libby checked it through: the punctuation, spelling and grammar were flawless.

Reading about Seth's morning routine, Libby realised how strange it was that she was working for, and living in the house of a man she'd never met, and had only spoken with once!

From watching videos of him and reading what he put online, it seemed like she knew a lot about Seth, but in reality, she knew she didn't. She was acutely aware social media portrayed a persona which could be far from the real human being behind it. But even if only a portion of what he posted were true, he was nothing like Libby. She wondered how they'd get on as boss and employee when they finally met. Would they clash? She certainly couldn't imagine them being friends.

Libby waded through emails, trying to stick firmly to Seth's instructions to only forward him messages she couldn't deal with herself.

After two hours of staring at the screen her head was beginning to ache so Libby decided to take a break and grab a quick caffeine hit.

Making a mental note to pick up some instant coffee so she could make herself a hot drink in her own little apartment, she went into the main kitchen. Looking out of the French doors, she spotted Jamie pruning a bush and tapped on the glass to get his attention. He straightened up, smiled, and beckoned to her to come outside and join him.

"What you up to out here?" Libby asked when she reached him.

"I was just finishing up on this side of the garden before moving on to the super exciting job of cleaning out the tool shed. I've been putting it off for ages, but today will be the day."

"Would you like a hot drink?" Libby offered. "I can make tea, but I've got no hope of getting a coffee out of that machine."

Jamie smiled in appreciation. "A tea would be great, thanks! Milk and one sugar, please."

Libby made them both drinks and took them outside. Jamie had put down his secateurs and was sat on the steps leading from the patio to the lawn. He indicated to Libby to join him.

"So, how are you finding things around here?" he asked.

"Okay, I think. It's all still a bit new and strange. I've never lived anywhere like this before."

"I don't think many people have, to be fair."

They both laughed.

"So where were you living before you came here?" Jamie asked.

"Not far from here. I shared a place with my boyfriend," Libby confessed. "But we broke up and thankfully this job with accommodation included was available."

"Sorry to hear about you and your boyfriend."

Libby took a sip of her tea. "Thanks," she said. "Where do you live?"

"I rent a flat by the river with my girlfriend, Amy."

"Nice."

"Seth actually owns the building and gives us a subsidised rate, otherwise I could never afford to live there."

A shadow suddenly fell on Libby, blocking the sun which had been gently warming her face.

"This looks very cosy," said a deep, stern voice.

Libby jumped and looked up. Standing in front of her was a man she immediately recognised as her employer, Seth Coleman. He was medium height, probably around five foot, ten, with very short dark hair, and wore blue jeans with white Nike trainers and a plain black t-shirt, which showed off his arm muscles to perfection.

Libby hurriedly stood up, spilling lukewarm tea over herself in the process.

"Mr Coleman, it's a pleasure to finally meet you," she said. "I'm Libby, your new personal assistant."

"I know who you are," Seth replied as his cold, green eyes appraised her. Libby's skin prickled under his gaze.

He checked his watch. "You can have five minutes to get changed before I need you in my study."

He didn't wait for Libby's response, but turned and walked swiftly back into the house.

"He's a little bit scary," Libby muttered.

Jamie laughed. "He's really not. He's just kind of serious and . . . intense about, well, most stuff. But he's a great boss."

"I'll choose to believe you," she said, downing the last gulp of tea from her mug.

She wasn't at all pleased with the impression she'd made on Seth. He wasn't to know that her goofing around with Jamie was the first break she'd taken today. And then she'd managed to throw her drink over herself. She mentally face-palmed. Good grief. He probably thought her lazy and clumsy.

Conscious of the short amount of time available for her to make herself presentable, Libby hurried into the house and to her bedroom where she swiftly changed into a clean shirt and trousers. She splashed cool water on her face, which was still flushed from the embarrassment of her pouring tea over herself.

Attempting to feel organised and on top of things, she grabbed a notepad and pen as she passed her desk and rushed to Seth's office, on the first floor.

She knocked on the closed office door and her employer's voice answered, "Come in."

If anything, this room was even more spartan than the rest of the house. There was no clutter anywhere. No pens lying around the desk or random pieces of paper, not even a photo of loved ones on the bookshelves, which instead contained a vast number of self-help books — all of which, Libby realised in horror, were shelved in alphabetical order. He'd probably have a fit if she saw the state of her office already. Libby made a mental note to give it a bit of a tidy as soon as she was finished here.

Seth was sitting behind his enormous glass desk. He indicated to Libby to take a seat. "It's nice to meet you, Libby," he said, glancing up from his computer with a distracted smile. "How are you finding the place? Got everything you need?"

"Yes, absolutely. Your house is amazing. Thank you," said Libby automatically, before stopping herself and saying, "Actually, my contract said I'd have use of a car. I was wondering if it would be possible to get that sorted soon?" Even after a few days, Libby had found it hard to be stuck on the Hill without any transport.

Seth looked surprised. She suspected he'd imagined his question was rhetorical; why on earth wouldn't Libby be happy working here? He replied, "Of course. Ask Jamie to give you the keys to the Merc."

"A Mercedes?!" blurted out Libby without thinking.

Seth looked faintly amused. "Just a little one," he said. "I hope it'll be alright for you."

"I'm sure it'll be fine," said Libby, still stunned. The last car she'd had access to was Robert's fifteen-year-old Ford Fiesta. This would most definitely be a step up and a much nicer driving experience. She'd never even sat in a Mercedes before.

"Any other issues?"

"No, thank you."

"Good, I need you to update my online calendar. I'll email you with some notes about it and we'll check in again at our weekly meeting."

Seth's tone indicated the end of the conversation. She'd been in his office for less than five minutes. She was still clutching her notepad and pen.

She didn't want Seth to see her chatting with Jamie again, so she waited until she heard her new boss go out before hurrying out to the garden to find him, who was clearing out the tool shed. He grinned when she explained about the Mercedes and was happy to stop work for a few minutes and get her the keys to the car.

Libby practically bounced up and down with excitement when she saw the black Mercedes coupé. She'd never been bothered about cars before, but this one was so beautiful and looked like it would be such fun to drive.

She waited until she was officially done with work for the day before grabbing the keys, heading back out to the garage and taking the car for a spin around Weybridge. It felt good to have the freedom to go out whenever she wanted again, and the car was a dream.

Libby was thankful not to have seen anything of Seth for the rest of that day. It seemed the only non-perk of her new job was her boss.

* * *

Seth didn't make an appearance when Libby came out of her apartment the following morning either. Libby's habit was already to gravitate to the kitchen as soon as she was ready for the day to have a chat with Sarah who'd make her a coffee. Libby wasn't absolutely sure this was okay for her to do — it was Seth's own kitchen after all — but she'd checked his very extensive folder of instructions and hadn't found anything to say it wasn't.

"Hello, Libby," said Sarah, cheerfully. "Cappuccino or latte this morning?"

"Morning, Sarah. A latte would be lovely, thanks."

Sarah started up the coffee machine.

"Have you seen Seth yet today?" Libby asked.

"No," replied Sarah. "But he will have been up for hours. I don't usually see him until bulletproof coffee time at eleven."

"What on earth is bulletproof coffee?"

Sarah laughed. "It's coffee with butter and MCT oil added to it."

Libby pulled a face.

"I know it sounds disgusting, and it looks it too actually, with all that fat floating on the top of it," said Sarah. "But Seth swears by it."

"Did his other personal assistants have breakfast in here? I'm worried I've overstepped a mark. Should I take my food to eat in my rooms?"

Sarah shrugged. "You're his first live-in PA, but I don't think Seth will be bothered. It's not like you're disturbing him. He usually eats in his office when he's at home."

"Okay, if you're sure."

Still not one hundred per cent comfortable, despite Sarah's assurances, Libby ate her breakfast quickly, taking the final sips of her coffee into her office. She wanted to get a head start on any changes to Seth's diary for the day. He made updates to it frequently, and she worried she was liable to get caught out if she didn't keep a close eye on it.

She already knew Seth only checked emails once a day at 9 a.m. She had to wait until then if she needed a reply.

There were also several hours a day blocked off on his calendar when Libby wasn't supposed to disturb him at all unless there was an 'absolute emergency'. As Libby found Seth rather intimidating, she felt relieved to be left to her own devices and work her way through her jobs for the day.

She began by checking her own emails, forwarding any which Seth would have to see before the 9 a.m. deadline, and scanning Seth's meetings. She made a note to herself: Seth's meetings for the day were all in the morning and lasted no longer than twenty minutes – good to be aware of if she was going to help manage his diary.

So she could get more of a heads-up about her employer, she'd read a ton of articles about him since starting the job and marvelled at the discipline of his routine: getting up at five every morning, spending the first hour of the day meditating and reading self-help books, before he then spent the next hour in his private gym working his way through programmes specially developed for him.

Breakfast was next — and was either an egg-white omelette or a protein smoothie, prepared by Sarah.

By the time Libby was due to clock in, Seth had done three writing sprints for his next book and was ready to check his emails.

Of course, despite knowing this in theory, Libby was surprised to discover that it appeared Seth really did stick to this routine, and it wasn't just for show.

The phone was busy all morning. Seth didn't have a landline telephone in his office and his business mobile was kept with Libby. Very few people had his private number, and anyone wanting to get through to him had to go through Libby, even his secretary at his property company, Belinda, which meant she had a lot of calls to field.

Libby was struggling to format a blog post properly when the house phone rang. "Hello?" she answered.

"Hi, who's this?" a male voice asked.

"I'm Libby, Seth's new PA. How can I help?"

"Oh, hi, Libby. Sorry, we haven't had a chance to meet yet. This is John. Can you put me through to Seth, love? I'm in a bit of a hurry."

"Sure, no problem," Libby replied, and transferred the call over to Seth's personal number.

About sixty seconds later, her own work mobile rang with Seth's number.

"Can you come up to my office, please? Straight away."

"Sure," said Libby, but Seth had already hung up.

She hurried up the stairs to his office, notepad and pen in hand, and knocked on the door.

She entered once she'd heard Seth's deep, "Come in."

Somehow Libby could tell Seth was angry even though all he was doing was sitting at his desk typing. When he looked up, his face showed he was furious.

"Why did you put a journalist through to my private number?" he barked.

"I didn't!" replied Libby automatically.

"So, who do you think it was that I was just talking to then?" Seth asked, slowly.

"John . . ." said Libby, realising at the exact moment what an idiot she'd been. "I'm so sorry, he said he knew you."

"And you didn't even ask for a surname or what company he was calling from?"

"No, I'm sorry."

"I explained to you how important it is that I'm not disturbed when I'm working. I thought I'd made myself clear on that point. And I especially don't want my private number being handed around the staff of the *Daily Mail*."

Libby felt herself go red. "I understand that. He wouldn't have your private number because I've made sure it doesn't show up if I transfer someone to you."

"That's something, I suppose!" Seth glared at her and opened his mouth as if to continue his tirade, but stopped himself. He rubbed his forehead with his fingers and seemed to take a deep breath before saying, "It's a classic trick journalists like to try. Don't fall for it again."

"I'll try not to," said Libby, stiffly.

She stormed back to her own office, only just stopping herself from slamming the door like a petulant teenager.

She knew she'd made a stupid mistake, but had it really been necessary for him to speak to her like that? So he was disturbed, for a minute — it was hardly the end of the world! And she'd explained that the journalist wouldn't have his private number.

She had half a mind to quit right there and then. She could call Melissa and take whatever temp job was available. But if she left this job, she was leaving her new home as well. And she hadn't even received her first pay cheque from Seth yet: she didn't have the money for a deposit on a flat, even if she knew of one available, which she didn't.

Melissa would immediately offer to have her stay, but it wasn't fair to her friend. Melissa's flat was small, and Libby had no idea of how long she'd need to be there.

She could stay with her parents. She knew they'd be delighted to welcome her back, but they lived in the middle of rural Somerset, not exactly the best base for job hunting.

But was she overreacting? Yes, Seth was rude, but he had explicitly asked her not to interrupt him. She'd messed up. He was a strict boss, but she liked her job and the perks of the lovely apartment and car that came with it. Plus, she generally didn't even seem to have to spend much face time with Seth. Was it really worth leaving over a few cross words?

Libby decided to focus on work and see how she felt at the end of the day.

* * *

Libby was finishing off an email as it approached 5 p.m. when she heard a knock at her door. "Come in!" she called out. She knew Jamie would be leaving about now, and she assumed he was popping his head in to say goodbye. She was surprised when the door opened to reveal Seth.

"Do you have a moment?" he asked stiffly. He looked supremely uncomfortable. The small amount of ire left in Libby contemplated telling him she was busy, but that would be childish and wouldn't achieve anything.

"Of course, what can I do for you?" she said instead.

"I think I owe you an apology," Seth replied.

Silence ensued. Libby would have filled it, but she'd been left speechless. She didn't know Seth well, but the little she did know hadn't prepared her for this eventuality in any way, shape or form. He definitely didn't seem like the sort of person to regularly admit he was in the wrong.

"Oh," she finally managed to say.

"Yes," Seth continued awkwardly. "It's your first week and I appreciate I have some unusual requests and working habits. It wasn't fair of me to pull you up on a mistake so harshly."

"Thank you for saying so," Libby replied.

"Anyway, I've updated my schedule. I'm leaving for Amsterdam early tomorrow. Just email me if you have any queries. Oh, the photos you sent over for the blog . . . very good."

And, without waiting for a response, Seth left.

CHAPTER 4

It really wasn't all that different in the house without Seth around. Libby did her best to follow his directions to the letter. Most of the work was basic admin, but there was also some research for the book Seth was writing, which was fun.

Sarah and Jamie had taken the opportunity of Seth being away to take a few days holiday. It was kind of nice to have the amazing house and gardens all to herself, but Libby couldn't relax — Seth might well return early from his trip, so she mainly kept to her own rooms.

She found the thought of spending the whole weekend alone in Seth's house didn't appeal, and she was glad she'd made plans with Melissa.

"Is Sunday evening still alright?" her friend asked when Libby called her to confirm. "I've been dying to see what lies beyond those gates."

"Sunday's fine. I'll give you the grand tour of my flat if you like," offered Libby, laughing, "And I'll even cook."

"I'll hold you to that!"

"Around 7?"

"Sounds good, see you then."

* * *

Libby grabbed her purse and car keys on Sunday afternoon. She still couldn't believe she got to drive a Mercedes whenever she wanted — it was crazy.

She drove off the Hill, using her key card at the entrance gate, and headed for the little community centre she went to for her yoga class at least twice a week. The centre was in a village a few miles outside of Weybridge. There were probably classes that would have been quicker for her to get to, but these were run by Libby's friend, Anna, who she'd met at her first temping job. Libby loved the array of characters always present at Anna's classes and the way her friend always tried to cater for everyone's individual needs.

Anna greeted Libby with a hug when Libby entered the slightly shabby hall where everyone was laying their yoga mats down.

"Congratulations on your new job," her tiny, raven-haired friend whispered, before turning her attention to the rest of the class.

Libby left the class feeling relaxed and thoroughly stretched out. She pulled out of the centre's tiny car park, and went to Morrisons. She wasn't really in the mood to cook properly, so she grabbed some posh pasta stuffed with spinach and ricotta, a pot of mascarpone, and a loaf of garlic ciabatta. As a nod towards health, she added a bag of salad leaves to the basket. She couldn't invite Melissa round and not offer her some sort of pudding — a couple of slices of chocolate cheesecake called to her.

She treated herself to some flowers too, and then a vase from the homeware section when she realised she didn't currently have anything she could put them in. They'd look lovely on the coffee table in her sitting room.

Libby still felt a bit like she'd been plucked out of her life: the life in which she worked random office jobs and lived in a small terraced house with her long-term boyfriend, but she was excited to show her friend around the fancy house she now called home.

* * *

The front gate buzzer went and Libby pressed the button to open it for her friend.

"Wow!" said Melissa, getting out of her car. "This place is amazing . . . Tell me that's not the 'little run-around' mentioned in the job spec!" she continued, clocking the Mercedes Libby had left parked outside the garage.

"It is!" replied Libby, grinning.

"Have you driven it yet?"

"Of course! Not very far admittedly, but it's amazing! Come and see inside the house."

They opened the bottle of Chablis Melissa had brought with her and Libby showed her around her rooms.

"This is gorgeous," Melissa said, enviously.

"I know, thank you so much for finding the job for me. I don't know what I would have done if you hadn't."

Melissa pulled her into a hug. "You could have stayed with me for as long as you'd needed. But even I have to admit my tiny flat is nowhere near as lovely as this place. I mean, look at your view!" She gestured towards one of the bedroom windows which faced a particularly beautiful part of the grounds. "It's great that you have your own door into the garden as well so you can come and go as you please without disturbing anyone."

"Yes, and it makes for a really short commute. I've even got a patio area," Libby said, opening up the door to her sitting room which led out to the garden. "Though I think it's a bit cold and drizzly to eat out there tonight."

"You're right, but it'll be gorgeous in the summer."

The evening with her friend was exactly what Libby needed. They talked for hours, sharing wine and food, and by the time Melissa left, Libby's apartment felt much more like home to her.

* * *

Libby began work on Monday morning with her head just a teeny bit sore and she was grateful to be living in such a calm, quiet space.

She was settling into work with a strong cup of instant coffee next to her when the gate buzzer went. As Libby was the only person in the house, she got up and pressed the intercom.

"Hello?" she said.

"Hi. Delivery for Mr Coleman."

"Okay," Libby replied and pressed the button to open the gate.

A van drove in and pulled up in front of the house and a tall, skinny dark-haired man of around fifty, wearing overalls, jumped out of the driver's seat and made his way to the passenger side. He lifted something out. It was only when he turned around to face Libby again that she could see he held a very wiggly puppy.

He went to pass the animal to Libby, who automatically took a step back. Sensing her confusion, he said, "I'm supposed to be delivering this little guy to Mr Coleman today."

"I'm Mr Coleman's assistant, and I can assure you, I know nothing about this."

"He's all paid for. I was just told to deliver," said the man. And before Libby could protest further, she found herself with the furry bundle and some paperwork in her arms. She opened her mouth but he called out, "Take it up with your boss, love," as he got back in his van and drove away.

Libby stood in shock as she processed what had happened: what was she supposed to do with a puppy? She looked down at her cargo, a golden ball of fluff.

She carried the dog inside and put it on the floor of her office while she grabbed her phone and called Seth — she hadn't forgotten she was only supposed to contact Seth in an emergency, but surely this counted as an emergency?

Seth's mobile went to voicemail. "Hi Seth, it's Libby. I have a bit of a situation here. Call me back as soon as you can, please. Bye."

She retrieved the puppy from her waste paper bin and wiped up a puddle of wee that had appeared. She needed somewhere safe to put him until she heard back from Seth.

She couldn't think with the puppy attacking everything. Her first thought was to let him out to play in the garden, but he was so little and wriggly, Libby was worried he might slip through a hole somewhere and either get lost or stuck. She had nothing for this dog at all — not even a collar and lead.

She waited for half an hour, but there was no response from Seth. Libby was determined to brave calling him again — she wasn't able to get any work done like this.

This time Seth's phone rang, and his voice snapped, "Yes?"

Libby took a deep breath before replying, "Hi Seth, so sorry to disturb you, but there's been a delivery of a puppy here . . ."

"A Golden Retriever puppy, that's right."

"So you were expecting it?"

"Yes. There's a note on the calendar."

Libby quickly switched her laptop screen over to the shared work calendar. There was indeed an entry for the morning labelled simply 'delivery'.

"You could have warned me a dog would be arriving!" said Libby, exasperated.

"I wasn't aware I had to check my purchase decisions with you," Seth replied, coldly.

"Of course, you don't, but I don't have anything for a dog."

"Libby, I'm about to speak in front of 5000 people. Take the credit card I've left you and buy the dog anything it needs."

"I don't know how to look after a puppy."

"Well, I suggest you learn quickly," Seth snapped, and the line went dead.

Libby swore at the phone. That arrogant *git!* This was completely unacceptable — how could she be expected to look after a puppy? But it sounded like she didn't have any choice: there was no one else around to do it. She'd show Seth she could deal with a crisis, but it was ridiculous.

She definitely needed a safe place to put the puppy and a collar and lead. Oh, and food. And a bowl. Two bowls actually, because he'd need one for water as well, wouldn't he?

Libby googled the nearest pet store. She couldn't safely have the puppy in her car with him wiggling about all over the place, so she emptied a deep plastic box off one of her office shelves, put a towel in the bottom, and popped the puppy in. No way was this little guy pooping in the only Mercedes she was ever likely to drive.

She put the puppy and his crate in the passenger footwell of the car and set off.

After twenty frantic minutes of trying to keep her eyes on the road and not on the puppy who was doing his best to escape the container, Libby pulled up outside the pet shop — it was the size of a supermarket, for goodness' sake. How much stuff did cats and dogs need?

The puppy had managed not to soil the box, thankfully. Libby picked him up and he snuggled down into her arms. Despite her irritation, she couldn't help smiling.

A sales assistant came over to fuss over the puppy as soon as Libby entered the store.

"Awwww!" exclaimed the young woman. "What's his name?"

"He doesn't have one yet," admitted Libby.

"Are you here to pick up a few things for him?"

"I'm here to pick up everything for him," Libby said. "He belongs to my boss who has absolutely nothing for a dog."

"Right then!" said the sales assistant, cheerfully. "Sounds like you'll need a trolley."

* * *

An hour later and Libby was back in the car, which now barely had enough room in it for her and the puppy. She had a crate for the car, a larger crate for the puppy to sleep in in the house, blankets, two beds, a regular collar and a glow-in-the-dark one, food and water bowls, dog food, dog treats, toys . . . the list seemed endless.

She felt a tiny pang of guilt at how much she'd charged to Seth's credit card but swiftly rebuked herself. He had plenty of money and had told her to spend some of it on this dog; a dog he'd chosen to have and which she was apparently stuck looking after. Anything she could buy to make life a bit easier at this point was money well spent.

It was much calmer driving back to Seth's house with the puppy safe in his crate. She parked the car by the garage and opened up the door to the crate so she could put his lead on and help him out. She grinned at how happy he was to be carried by her.

The paperwork she'd been given with the puppy was lying on Libby's desk. She had a quick read-through of it while she sat on the floor with the puppy sleeping on her lap — the excitement of the pet store must have tired him out.

Apparently, he was twelve weeks old and he'd had his first vaccinations already. He was also Kennel Club registered, whatever that meant.

Libby took the opportunity of five minutes' peace to slip into her flat and make herself a coffee. Then she set to some research: she had all the puppy gear and no idea, but that was about to change.

CHAPTER 5

The next morning, the puppy was absolutely adamant that 6 a.m. was time to get up and no amount of Libby ignoring him would convince him otherwise. Libby had set his crate up in her sitting room the night before, so she could hear him if he wasn't happy, but after an hour of him crying, she moved him into her bedroom. She told him firmly that he was staying in his crate though, she wasn't going to have puppy pee on her bed, and he seemed to accept this compromise.

At 6.20 a.m. Libby gave in and got up. She took the puppy into the garden and fed him one of his four meals of the day (she'd had to set reminders on her phone for all of them). Then she emailed Seth so he'd see it when he did his daily email check. She didn't know what the puppy should be called and everything she'd read said it was really important to get your dog used to its name as early as possible.

Libby had her breakfast, showered and dressed and took the puppy outside again for a run around. She'd learnt during a puppy care cramming session the evening before he wouldn't be able to go for a proper walk until he'd had his second lot of vaccinations.

It was raining, but that didn't seem to bother the little dog who happily nosed around and seemed to pee on everything he came into contact with.

When it was time for Libby to start work, she headed back inside to clear everything she could off the floor of the office and make sure the puppy's bed was comfy for him. She didn't envisage being able to get much work done again, but she'd give it her best shot.

She logged into her emails again and swiftly opened the one from Seth. *Call him whatever you want*, it said.

Libby grinned to herself, deep down she'd been hoping that would be Seth's response.

"Barney!" she called in her most cheerful, enticing voice. "Come!" She was thrilled when Barney stopped chewing on his paw and came padding over to her. "Good boy!" she exclaimed.

* * *

The following morning, Libby took Barney into the garden before starting work. Sarah was back, and Seth was due to return from Amsterdam in the afternoon. As she followed the puppy around his sniffing spots, Libby waved to her friend in the kitchen. Spotting Barney, Sarah's eyes widened and she put down the sweet potato she was peeling, wiped her hands, and came out to join them.

"And who are you?" Sarah asked, bending down to pet the puppy.

"His name's Barney," Libby said.

"How did you convince Seth to let you have a puppy?"

"I didn't. Barney's his."

"Seriously?"

"Yep. He was delivered a couple of days ago. I thought there must have been a mistake, but apparently not."

Sarah frowned, nonplussed. "Why would Seth want a dog?"

"I have absolutely no idea," replied Libby. "But he sure is cute. He was delivered a couple of days ago. I thought there must have been a mistake when this random bloke turned up out of nowhere and dumped a puppy on me."

"Didn't Seth let you know a dog would be arriving?"

"There was a mention in the diary of a delivery . . . that was the only heads-up I had."

"That's so typical of Seth," said Sarah, with an affectionate shake of the head.

"Thankfully Barney's only had one accident so far and seems to be almost house trained, so it could be a lot worse I suppose," Libby said, laughing.

"Seth doesn't mean to be selfish," Sarah said. "He's just not very good at thinking about other people. It wouldn't occur to him to check with you or to wonder how you'd manage with a puppy, or even what's really involved in looking after a puppy. He needs things pointed out to him. He doesn't do subtlety."

"I'm going to have to say something," said Libby. "Barney takes a lot of looking after, and he's rather distracting."

"I bet he is!" said Sarah, as Barney ran around her legs.

"I'm just hoping Seth's planning to take over with him sometime soon."

"I wouldn't count on it!" Sarah replied.

* * *

A few hours of attempting to work with a puppy nibbling at her ankles later, Libby was on her way to pick up Seth from Gatwick Airport, humming along to Christmas songs on the radio. Barney was safe in his crate in the back of the car.

Libby had checked already that Seth's flight was on time, but she confirmed it again once she'd parked. She knew Seth wouldn't be long coming through Arrivals; he had only taken a carry-on bag. Libby messaged to let him know where she was parked and she had only been waiting a few minutes when she spotted Seth marching purposefully through the terminal doors, talking into his hands-free set. She got out of the car and waved so he'd see where she was. He raised his eyebrows in amusement and she blushed and stopped abruptly. Why did he always make her feel like such an idiot?

"How was your flight?" Libby asked when he'd reached the car and she could see he'd finished his conversation.

"It was fine," Seth replied. "Thank you," he added.

Barney gave a welcoming woof, making Seth jump as he opened the passenger door.

"Is that the dog?" he asked.

Libby bit back the sarcastic reply forming in her mouth. "Yep," she said, climbing into the driver's seat. "This is Barney."

"Barney," Seth repeated, mulling it over. "Good name," he concluded, getting into the car.

"Thanks."

"Why is he in the Mercedes though?"

"He's only twelve weeks old."

"That sounds like a very good reason for him not to be in the Mercedes," Seth retorted. He turned his attention to his mobile phone.

"He can't be left by himself yet," Libby replied. "And Sarah wouldn't have been able to get much done with Barney around."

"Hmmm . . ." said Seth, noncommittally. "Is he trained?"

"He's almost house-trained," Libby said.

Seth raised an eyebrow. "Does he sit and . . . um . . . heel?" he asked.

"Well . . . no," said Libby.

Seth didn't comment and continued to focus on his phone.

"He only arrived a couple of days ago," Libby continued. "I haven't had much time to train him yet . . . To be honest, I don't really know much about training a puppy. It wasn't exactly in the job description when I applied."

"Libby?"

"Yes?" Libby replied nervously, worried she'd gone too far.

"Do you think you could start the car?"

"Oh, right, sure, sorry," Libby mumbled and focused on driving back to St George's Hill.

* * *

Libby was woken up early again the next morning by Barney whining to be let out for a pee. She crawled groggily out of bed and opened the door to the puppy's crate. He came bouncing out and ran straight to the patio doors. Libby pulled on her trainers and a coat before opening them and going out with him. He only needed a minute before he was wanting to head back indoors; it was drizzling again and he knew breakfast was next on the agenda.

As Barney had gobbled up his food, and the kettle was boiling for Libby's first coffee of the day, he began to bark. Libby groaned and half-heartedly shushed him as she added a spoonful of instant coffee powder to her mug.

Barney continued to bark, his tail wagging hard the whole time, and he ran to the patio doors. In her tired, early morning state Libby couldn't have closed them properly, and Barney pushed them open and ran straight outside.

"Barney, no!" Libby shouted, grabbing her shoes and yanking them on again.

She raced outside after the puppy only to find him with a bemused Seth, who was tentatively stroking Barney's head.

Seth's hair was wet, and he was dressed in workout gear — a stark white, rather tight t-shirt and black tracksuit bottoms — and was, presumably, on the way back from the swimming pool.

"Hi," he said, awkwardly. "I think he wanted to say hello . . ."

"I guess so," Libby replied, freezing and feeling self-conscious in her ancient heart-covered pyjamas. She crossed her arms across her chest, wishing she was wearing a bra.

He abruptly shifted subject. "There's a conference I'd like you to attend with me in January. It's in Barcelona. You need to make hotel and flight bookings asap."

"No problem," said Libby, willing the conversation to end.

"I didn't realise you were such an early riser," Seth commented.

"I'm not usually," she said, unable to keep the snap out of her tone.

"Oh, right . . . well, I'd better get to my workout . . . Nice PJs, by the way." And with that, Seth continued into the house.

Libby scooped up Barney and stomped back into her kitchen. Why did she always have to make such a fool of herself in front of her employer? Wandering round his garden in these ridiculous pyjamas... And why was he so infuriating? She was amazed he was continuing to put up with her, to be honest, and amazed at herself that she hadn't handed in her notice yet. Not that she was planning to stay much longer anyway, she reminded herself. Seth's demands were completely unreasonable — expecting her to look after a puppy, for goodness' sake. Then she realised she was still cuddling said puppy, and absentmindedly kissing his head. Barney wriggled, and Libby bent to put him down. He went off, busily hunting around for his toys and she picked up her phone resolutely: she'd call Melissa now and ask her to find her another position.

But, looking around the room, she felt a pang of regret about how much she'd miss it if she left. She'd never lived anywhere like this before, and probably wouldn't again. Not having to share her space with roommates was an added benefit: if she moved out, she'd more than likely only be able to afford a room in a grotty house share, at least to begin with. And she would really like to go to Barcelona . . .

She put down her mobile. As cross as she was feeling with Seth, she had too much to lose if she left. Libby guessed she'd give her boss one more chance to prove he wasn't the unreasonable, unfeeling, cold man of business she suspected he was.

Seth was out at a conference in London for the whole of the next day and left before Libby began work. She worked her way through her list as usual and was about to stop to have a bite of lunch with Sarah when her office phone rang.

"Hello?" she answered.

"Hello, that doesn't sound like Maria," said a male voice.

"I'm Libby, Seth's new personal assistant. I think Maria must have been my predecessor." (*One of my many predecessors, from the sound of things*, Libby thought.) "How can I help you?"

"I hope you're fitting in well up there at Whitehaven. I'm Lennon, Seth's father," the man said. "I've been abroad and haven't seen Seth for quite a while. I was wondering if you could find some time in my son's very busy schedule for him to have a cup of tea with his old dad."

Libby's thoughts immediately flew to her messing up when the reporter called. "That sounds lovely," she said. "I will just need to do some checks though to confirm you are who you say you are."

"Of course, very sensible. What would you like to know?"

Libby pulled up the folder in her computer containing scanned copies of Seth's ID documents. She opened the one containing his birth certificate.

"You said your name was?"

"It's Lennon, Lennon Worth. My parents were Beatles fans. Seth took his mother's surname."

A quick check of the certificate confirmed Seth's father's name was indeed Lennon Worth.

"And what hospital was Seth born in?" Libby asked, just to be extra careful.

"The North Middlesex," Lennon replied, immediately.

"Great," said Libby, smiling and trying to imagine what Seth's father would be like. His voice was certainly similar to his son's, if a little sharper perhaps.

"Just half an hour one day would be fine," Lennon said. "I know he's got a lot on."

"How about Wednesday at 3 p.m.? Are you okay to meet him at the house?" Libby suggested.

"I don't drive, I'm afraid. I'll be coming by train."

"No problem, I can pick you up from Weybridge station at 2.45?"

"That sounds perfect," replied Lennon. "But can you not let him know it's me? I want it to be a surprise."

"Absolutely," said Libby, and put the booking in the calendar.

* * *

Seth didn't mention the unspecified meeting added to his Wednesday afternoon and Libby delighted in keeping the secret. She was excited to meet Seth's father; it felt a little like gaining another bit in the puzzle of figuring out her boss.

She took Barney with her to pick up Lennon: she liked to have the company, and he seemed to enjoy the drive.

Only one person was waiting outside Weybridge station, and it was a tall man who looked around sixty, so Libby guessed he was Lennon, though his height, unkempt hair and large belly meant he didn't resemble his son at all. She pulled up in front of him and opened the window. "Hello, are you Lennon?" she asked.

"I most certainly am!" said the man cheerfully. "And you must be Libby."

"Yes, hop in and you'll be with Seth in no time. I can't wait to see his face."

A shadow seemed to fall over Lennon's own face at her remark. "Don't worry," she quickly added. "You're all booked into the diary, I'm sure he'll be thrilled to see you."

Lennon opened the passenger door to get in and Barney emitted a little growl. Lennon jumped.

"Barney!" said Libby. "I'm sorry, Lennon, he's never done that before. It must be because he's in his crate and can't get out to give you a proper welcome."

Lennon looked wary, but it was clear Barney was only a puppy and contained in his crate so he got into the car.

* * *

Libby was very grateful when they arrived back at Seth's house. Barney had paced his crate, letting out low growls the whole journey back. Lennon had clearly felt uncomfortable and Libby couldn't blame him. She couldn't imagine what had got into the usually friendly puppy.

"Blimey," muttered Lennon, eyeing the house.

"Haven't you visited here before?" Libby asked.

"Er, no. I'm afraid me and Seth haven't been close for a while. But hopefully this visit will change that."

"I'll just put the dog inside," she said and she put a lead on Barney and marched him into the crate in her office, much to his chagrin. "It'll only be for a little while," she whispered gently. "We can't have you being so fierce you frighten our guests."

Libby rejoined Lennon and led him into the house and up the stairs to Seth's office.

"Hi," Seth said cheerfully when he saw Libby, but his face darkened when he recognised the man standing behind her. "What are you doing here?" he barked at his father, standing up.

"I just wanted to see you, son," said Lennon, sounding hurt. Libby looked from one man to the other trying to work out what was going on here. A feeling of dread built in her stomach: it seemed she'd made a huge mistake not checking with Seth himself before making the appointment his dad had requested.

"How much do you need?" snapped Seth.

"I didn't come here for money," said Lennon.

"Then you can just go. You know I don't have anything to say to you." Seth turned back to his computer.

Libby didn't know what to do. She was surprised that Seth would treat his father like this. The man may be a little robotic at times, but she hadn't believed he could be so cold and unfeeling, especially to his own father.

"Don't be like that, son . . ."

"You do not get to call me 'son'," Seth hissed, advancing on him. "Libby, could you please ring for an Uber to take my father back to wherever he's referring to as his home at the moment? He can wait outside until it arrives."

"Listen, Seth . . ." Lennon began.

"If you want something, just ask," snapped Seth, his face set.

"Well, I am a little strapped for cash . . ."

Seth gave a humourless laugh. "I knew it!"

"I wouldn't need much . . ."

"How much?"

"A thousand. Two, tops."

Wordlessly, Seth went to one of the drawers on the side of his desk. He took out three bundles of fifty-pound notes. "Take three grand," he said, pushing them across the table. "Maybe the extra will mean I get a longer respite before you come begging again."

Libby's mouth dropped open. "Could you ring for that Uber, please, Libby?" repeated Seth, more softly.

"I can drive him . . ." Libby offered.

"I don't want you in a car with him," Seth said, sharp again. Something in his tone told Libby not to argue.

It wasn't like Libby to agree to something without knowing the reason why, but, despite his off-hand behaviour, she trusted Seth. She might not know why he wanted her to stay away from Lennon, but she'd respect his wishes.

Lennon looked utterly defeated.

"Goodbye," said Seth, pointing to the door.

Lennon turned and walked out of the office.

"I'll book the Uber," Libby said, and swiftly made her own exit.

Downstairs, she heard Lennon go straight out of the front door and close it firmly behind him.

Libby let Barney out of his crate and called Uber. Should she go outside and talk to Lennon while he waited? It seemed unbelievably rude to leave him out there by himself, but Seth had been very clear that he didn't want her around Lennon. What could have happened between the two of them to make Seth react that way to his father? Was it because his father was always asking for money? Libby had been shocked when Lennon had done so, but maybe he'd been desperate. It did sound like something he did a lot though, which must be difficult for Seth. But did he really resent helping his dad out? It couldn't be just about the money Lennon was asking for; a few thousand pounds was small change for Seth, and he was unfailingly generous with other things — her wage, for one. There must be something else that had made Seth behave the way he did.

Thankfully the Uber didn't take long to arrive. The driver buzzed for her to open the gate and she went out into the entrance hall to do so. Then, as she turned to go back into her office, she saw Seth standing at the top of the stairs watching his father, presumably wanting to ensure he wasn't going to come back inside and try to speak to him again.

He caught Libby's eye. "Could you come back up here when he's gone, please?" he asked.

"Of course."

Libby hung around for a couple of minutes, playing tug of war with Barney in the hall until she checked the camera and saw the Uber had left the property and then she pressed the button to close the gates.

She put Barney in his crate, took a deep breath to steel herself and went back up to Seth's office.

"Hi, Libby," said Seth as she came in through the open door. "Take a seat."

Libby sat down nervously. How angry was he going to be with her? She knew she should have checked with him about making the appointment. She'd allowed herself to be taken in. Again. At least this time the person was actually Seth's father, but she realised it could have been anyone wanting to get into Seth's home. It could have been a newspaper reporter again or even a crazed fan . . . She'd never worked for anyone in the public eye before, and it showed. She'd really have to tighten up on how she behaved towards people she hadn't met before especially when it came to them being invited into Seth's home. That's if he allowed her to keep her job.

"I'm really sorry," Libby blurted out before Seth could begin.

Seth nodded.

"And it won't happen again," she continued.

"It can't happen again," stressed Seth. "Not just with my father, but anyone I haven't authorised to come into my home."

She gulped hard. "Of course."

"I'm sorry you had to witness my father and me. It's always very . . . difficult when I see him."

"You must have your reasons for treating him the way you did."

"I do, and they're private," snapped Seth. He took a deep breath. "Sorry."

"Don't worry," said Libby. "Are you okay? Is there anything I can do?"

"I'm fine."

They stared at each other. Libby wondered if he was going to share any more with her, but it seemed he'd decided not to.

As she continued to look at him, it was as if she could feel the waves of hurt coming off him, however much she was sure he'd deny it. Whatever had happened between him and his father, it didn't seem that Seth was in any hurry to confide in her. The more Libby was getting to know her boss, the more complicated and unlike her first impressions of him he was.

CHAPTER 6

As the following weekend approached, Libby realised she could do with getting away for a couple of days. Her flat was lovely, and the work was fine, and interesting at times, but living and working in the same place meant she was feeling claustrophobic.

She hadn't been to visit her parents in Somerset since the summer and knew they'd be thrilled to have the opportunity to make a fuss of her. She decided to drive there when she'd finished work on Friday and come back after supper on Sunday.

The only thing she was worried about now was Barney. Of course, Barney was Seth's dog, not hers, and she knew she was being daft, but did Seth have any idea how to look after a puppy? Then again, up until a few days ago, she hadn't known anything about caring for a dog, so she was hardly one to talk.

She considered taking Barney with her to her parents' house, but it was a long drive, and her dad was allergic to dogs. There was also no knowing what Barney would decide to chew on once he was there.

It seemed ridiculous to email Seth to check he was happy for her to take the car for the weekend when he was sitting a few rooms away from her, but it seemed that was the way he wanted things and he was the boss, so who was she to argue?

She was saved from having to send an email and wait twenty-four hours for a response when she noticed she had a twenty-minute meeting with Seth booked into the calendar that afternoon.

Deciding Seth probably wouldn't want Barney running around his office while they talked, Libby put the puppy in his crate before going up to Seth's office with her notepad and pen. She knocked on the door and opened it after hearing the usual gruff "Come in".

Seth was on the phone and signalled to her to take a seat.

Libby doodled on her pad until Seth had finished. She couldn't help smiling at how frustrated he clearly was because his phone call had gone over the allotted time by about three minutes.

"Libby, hi," he said eventually.

He glanced down at her notebook. "I've been meaning to ask, is your iPad broken?"

"No, I just prefer using pen and paper."

"Oh . . . fair enough. Anyway, I thought it might be a good idea to check you're all up to date with our trip to Barcelona in January, and if you have any questions?"

"No, it all seems quite straightforward," Libby replied. "I've booked the flights and the hotel, and I'm in touch with the organiser of the conference you'll be speaking at."

"Great. There'll be a few things I'll want to fit in during the trip, so I'll email them over. Could you get a potential itinerary to me as soon as possible, please?"

"Sure. I'll have it to you tomorrow afternoon. Also, I'm hoping to visit my parents this weekend and I was wondering if I could use the Mercedes to drive there?"

"That's fine," Seth replied. "It's yours to use whenever you need it."

He looked at his laptop screen for a moment. "That's all I think. Everything's going well, I take it? No problems?"

"Well, unexpectedly having a puppy arrive has been more than a little distracting . . ."

"So I hear . . ." Seth said. Libby wasn't sure whether he meant Barney had been noisy or that Sarah had said something to him. "I understood the puppy would arrive house and crate trained."

"He did," said Libby, quickly, worried Seth would declare Barney was to be returned to the breeders the next day. "But he still wakes me up early, and it's difficult to focus on work when he's running around my feet and chewing on charging cables. And who's going to look after him this weekend, while I'm away?"

"I see," said Seth. He went silent. Libby wondered whether he was waiting for her to speak, or whether he was thinking over what she'd said. It turned out to be the latter.

"What if Jamie helped out?" he finally suggested. "If he's happy to dog-sit the puppy this weekend, tell him he can either have it as overtime or add the days to his holiday. He could have the puppy in the garden with him sometimes while you work."

"That's great for this weekend, and for the help when I'm working. The only problem is, Barney needs to be kept on a lead in the garden. It's not completely secure and while he is learning to come back when I call, I'm worried he'll run off."

"Let's secure it then," said Seth, simply. "We'll put a fence and gates cutting off the front from the back and have the rest of the back perimeter checked to make certain it's secure."

"That would be brilliant," Libby replied. Her life would be so much easier if she knew Barney couldn't escape when he went outside.

"Make some calls this afternoon, and tell them it's urgent," said Seth. "Anything else?"

"I think that's everything."

"Good. As soon as the new fencing is up, Jamie can take over some of the dog-watching duties."

* * *

Libby went to release Barney from his crate and decided to go and speak to Jamie, who was finally back from his holidays.

Looking impossibly bronzed for the time of year and even more handsome than usual, Jamie fell in love with Barney immediately.

"Of course, I'll look after him for a couple of days!" he exclaimed when Libby asked her favour. "It's no problem. In fact, it would be a pleasure." He picked the puppy up and delighted in Barney endeavouring to lick him excitedly. "And if the garden isn't secured by Monday, my sister's got a large pen she used for her puppy. I'm sure she'll let me borrow it until it's safe for the little guy to run around off-lead."

"Thanks, Jamie," Libby replied. "I'll make some phone calls now and see how quickly I can get someone to come out and sort the fencing."

She walked back to her office with Barney, looking forward to speaking to her mum and dad to let them know she was coming to visit and relieved she knew Barney would be safe while she was away.

Looking through the house folder, Libby found the list of trusted tradespeople and began calling around, all the time wondering why anyone would spend so much money on a dog they'd chosen but didn't seem particularly bothered about having.

* * *

At 8 p.m. on Friday evening, Libby arrived at her parents' bungalow. They'd waited to eat with her, and her mum, Margaret, had made Libby's favourite supper, lasagne.

Libby changed into some of the old, comfy clothes she kept at her parents' home, and fell upon the delicious food — the comfort of the familiar and the memories of happy meals past that it evoked making it even tastier.

After they'd finished eating, they moved into the sitting room and watched the news together.

"The Christmas tree lights are being switched on in Frome tomorrow evening if you fancy going along to see?" Margaret suggested.

"That sounds lovely, Mum," Libby replied. "Is the Christmas market going to be there as well?"

"Yes, and the male voice choir singing carols."

"Brilliant," said Libby, smiling.

Libby's family home might have been a little old-fashioned, and certainly wasn't as fancy as Seth's, but Libby found it wonderful to be around people who loved her, and she felt herself properly relax for the first time since the fateful morning when she'd walked in on Robert and his lover.

Her mind wandered to what would happen if Seth were in the room now, and she gave a little smile — he wouldn't be able to resist whipping her easy-going parents into shape, she thought.

As if she could tell exactly what her daughter was thinking about, Margaret asked her, "Tell us about your new job. What's your boss like?"

"He's okay," said Libby, carefully. She knew her parents worried about her lack of career and direction; they definitely thought she should be more than a personal assistant. "I don't see him very much. He works in his office, so I just get on with whatever he needs me to do," she continued. "I'm going to Barcelona with him in the new year."

Why was she not being honest about Seth? He could be a nightmare to work with, yet she found herself being relatively nice about him.

"You loved it there when you visited during your gap year, didn't you?" said her dad, Alan.

"Yeah, I did! I can't wait to go back."

"Have you heard anything from Robert?" Margaret asked.

"No, Libby said. She hadn't told her parents all the details of her break-up with Robert. It was all still too raw to share over the telephone. "Turns out, he was seeing someone else," she admitted.

"Oh no!" Margaret said, her hand flying to her mouth. "I can't believe it."

Alan moved over to hug his daughter. "I'm so sorry, sweetheart."

"Thanks, Dad," Libby said. "I'm fine, really. My new place is amazing, and you saw the car I get to drive."

"So, are you seeing this job as something you want to do long-term, or more of a stop-gap?" Margaret asked.

"I don't know yet," replied Libby, doing her best not to be annoyed by her mother's questioning. She'd just left a serious relationship and had been lucky enough to land a job with a home included, surely it was alright for her to take a bit of time to recalibrate and heal before making plans for the future? But then, at her age, her mother had already been married for two years and had been working as an English teacher at the same school since leaving university. Her future had been secure and set, whereas Libby's felt anything but.

* * *

The weather was fine the next morning. Libby had a lie in to make up a little bit for her Barney-induced early mornings and then took the opportunity to go walking with her camera and capture some of the beautiful local scenery.

Her mum didn't bring up Libby's future plans again when they had lunch together — Libby wondered if her dad had asked her not to.

Libby had seen no need to bring her work mobile to Somerset with her, as she'd only be there for the weekend. She had remembered her own phone though and had given her number to Jamie, who sent her regular updates and photos of Barney. The puppy seemed to be having a lovely time and was being delightfully spoilt by the looks of things.

Libby had to admit that, as exhausting as caring for Barney was, she did miss him. She refrained from regaling her parents with Barney pictures — she could just imagine her mother's reaction to discovering her daughter was being used as an unofficial dogsitter. But if being in charge of Barney was what it took to keep a comfortable roof over her head, for the time being, Libby was willing to accept those terms. Quite happily, in fact – Barney was her favourite part of the job some days.

She arranged to meet up with her mum and dad later and set off once again after lunch with her camera equipment in her rucksack.

Not fancying taking more nature photos, Libby drove to Frome and wandered the narrow streets, photographing anything that caught her eye, especially the Christmas stalls and the huge, decorated tree in the centre of the town, before meeting her parents.

The three of them wandered around the stalls for an hour, enjoying the first warming mulled wines and mince pies of the season. Libby bought Barney some homemade treats from a natural dog food stall, as well as a squeaky elf toy she'd put away for Christmas.

Then at 5 p.m., the choir sang 'Silent Night' and the mayor switched on the Christmas lights. It was just as Libby remembered it from her childhood.

* * *

Margaret put the kettle on as soon as they got home and Alan made a start on supper.

"Let me dump my camera stuff upstairs," Libby said. "I'll be back down in a minute."

While Libby was in her room that she heard the doorbell ring and thought nothing of it, assuming it was a parcel being delivered or a neighbour popping by. Her mum had just opened the front door as Libby came back downstairs.

"Is Libby Spellman here?" she heard a deep voice ask. A voice Libby immediately recognised as Seth's.

"Ah, there you are!" Seth continued, spotting Libby. His face was thunderous. "I've been trying to call you since 9 a.m. this morning."

"What are you doing here?" Libby asked, incredulously.

"It's the weekend . . ." said Margaret, her face expressing her puzzlement.

"I told you where I was going," Libby added.

"Why haven't you got your phone on you?" Seth asked.

"I have," Libby replied, pulling her mobile out of the back pocket of her jeans.

Seth glared at it. "Your work phone," he snapped, producing her work mobile from his own pocket. "I found it on your desk."

Libby's dad came out from the kitchen, wiping his hands on a tea towel. "Is everything alright out here?" he asked.

"Everything's fine, Dad," said Libby, embarrassment coursing through her. "This is my boss, Seth Coleman."

Before her dad could comment, Libby turned back to Seth.

"I'm on holiday. I'm not working," she reiterated. "Why would I bring my work phone with me?"

"In case I needed to contact you."

"I don't recall there being anything in my contract stating that you could contact me on a work-related matter when I wasn't actually working."

"I told you you'd need to be flexible," countered Seth.

"I didn't realise that meant I needed to be available to you even when I was on holiday."

"That doesn't sound very reasonable to me," piped up Margaret.

"Have you got any idea how many hours I have wasted today trying to hunt you down?" said Seth, huffily. "I only found this address because you've got your parents down as your next-of-kin." The steam seemed to have been blown out of his anger.

"You would have saved a lot of time and effort if you'd just spoken to Jamie. He's looking after Barney and so he has my number . . ." Seeing the blank look on Seth's face she added, "You know, Barney? Your dog?"

"You don't know your own dog's name?" Margaret blurted out.

Libby took a deep breath. "Mum, Dad, maybe it would be better if Seth and I sorted this out between ourselves."

"Of course, sorry, love," Margaret said. "Why don't you go into the living room. I'll bring you both through some coffee. How do you take yours?" she asked Seth as she left.

"Black, please," Seth replied. Now that his initial fury was waning, he appeared completely discombobulated, presumably he hadn't expected to be drinking coffee in a bungalow in Somerset on a Saturday evening.

He followed Libby into her parents' living room. She tried to imagine it through his eyes. She'd have thought he'd look down on it with the little knick-knacks dotted around among Libby's school photos, but he seemed quite at ease as he took the seat she offered him on one of the sofas.

"Seth, I really don't think it's acceptable for you to follow me to my parents' house!" Libby hissed. "What's the emergency that you had to drive all the way here and disturb my holiday for?"

"My talk in Barcelona has been moved so we need to fly out a day early now."

"I've already sorted that. Belinda emailed me about it on Friday. It's all in order."

"Well, that's good then." He shifted in his seat.

Margaret came in and handed Seth and Libby their coffees. "Right," said she said, breaking the tension. "If that's all sorted out, would you like to stay for supper, Seth?" There was still a trace of Margaret's indignation on behalf of her daughter laced into her invitation.

"No, thank you," replied Seth, standing up. "I appreciate the offer, but I have a considerable amount of work to catch up on."

Libby was surprised to feel a little wave of disappointment. Seth turning up like that had to go down in the top ten of weird things that had ever happened to her. Surely she didn't want her boss gate-crashing her break away, especially when he'd arrived in such a foul mood? What would they even find in common to talk about while they ate? What would her easy-going father make of her schedule-obsessed employer?

But she couldn't deny the fact that after she watched him drive away, she felt inexplicitly out of sorts for the rest of the evening.

* * *

Libby drove back to Surrey after supper and a lecture from her parents about setting boundaries with her employer on Sunday night, let herself into the house, and went straight to bed. She missed Barney's presence in her bedroom and looked forward to seeing him when Jamie brought him into work the next morning.

She was up early on Monday and thought she'd take the opportunity to go for a swim before breakfast. She was always meaning to start exercising properly, and with an indoor swimming pool and fully equipped gym at her disposal, she really had no excuse not to.

Having access to Seth's timetable definitely had its advantages at times: she knew he only used the pool on Tuesdays, Thursdays and Saturdays, so it would be completely free for her now.

Libby put on her swimming costume and then wrapped herself in her big, fluffy pink dressing gown to keep her covered and warm while she walked to the pool building. She didn't need anything else, she thought gleefully: the pool was fully stocked with thick, white towels, and she suspected the shampoo and conditioner in the showers there was considerably better than her own.

The new fence and gate were already up she noticed as she walked through the garden. It would be great to be able to let Barney wander around off-lead safe in the knowledge that he couldn't escape.

Five minutes later, and Libby was swimming laps. The water was crystal clear and the perfect temperature. What a treat to be in a salt-water pool without the harsh chlorine smell – bliss!

Libby floated on her back, looking up at the cloud-peppered sky through the building's glass ceiling. She concentrated on her breathing, trying to remember any tips she'd gleaned from random yoga classes over the years. She needed all the calm she could cram in before dealing with Seth and his demands later. Goodness only knew what sort of mood he'd be in with her after what had happened at her mother's house.

In and out, in and out. She was surrounded by calm . . .

Libby was pulled from her meditation by the sound of a man clearing his throat. "Good morning," said Seth.

Libby's eyes shot open, and she stood up in the water, grateful that it was deep enough to come up to her neck and so cover her swimsuit-clad body.

"Hi! I'm so sorry. It said in the folder I could use the pool, and I didn't think you used it at this time," she said, flustered.

"I don't usually," Seth said. "But I missed my swim this weekend so thought I'd get it in now. Don't worry, the pool's plenty big enough for both of us."

He took off his bathrobe and dropped it on the sun lounger. Libby realised she was staring — he had a very good body, but then he should have with all the exercise he did. Did everyone have that many abs?

She shook her head and began swimming again, carefully keeping to one half of the pool, watching Seth glide through the water out of the corner of her eye. He was a fantastic swimmer, of course he was. Libby considered getting out now he was here, but surely that would seem churlish. And the walk to where the towels were suddenly seemed excruciatingly long now that she'd have to walk past Seth in her swimming costume in order to get to it.

Ordinarily, Libby was pretty happy with her body, and it didn't bother her to wander around a pool or at the beach in her swimwear, but doing so in front of her boss was another matter, especially when her boss was a fitness fanatic. So she kept swimming and did her best to ignore Seth's presence.

Suddenly she heard a huge splash. She stopped mid-stroke and turned round: was Seth dive bombing at the other end of the pool?! No. Libby's heart stopped. It was Barney. He'd plunged into the pool and dropped like a stone; he'd never been in water before. She glanced at Seth and, unspoken, they both began swimming frantically to where the dog had jumped in, but Barney's head popped out of the water and he gave a happy bark and began doggy-paddling towards Libby.

"What the hell is a dog doing in my pool?" Seth shouted.

"I have no idea," said Libby, grabbing Barney's collar. "I didn't let him in, did I? I've been in here with you. And it's not just any dog, it's *your* dog."

"I don't care whose bloody dog it is. I want it out of my pool! The whole thing will need to be drained, cleaned and refilled now!"

Libby carried Barney out of the water via the side steps, no longer caring what Seth thought of her body. She grabbed her dressing gown and pulled it on, wrapping a towel round the soaking puppy, and marched out of the building.

It wasn't until her feet touched grass that Libby remembered she'd left her sandals which she'd worn to walk to the pool back inside. Well, she wasn't going to go back in, so she'd just have to make her way across the lawn in her bare feet. Wasn't that grounding? She was sure she'd read it was supposed to be very good for stress. She could definitely do with some stress relief now. It would probably be more effective if it wasn't so freezing cold.

Poor, confused Barney was so excited to see Libby, he was trying to lick her face. She stopped and stroked his head.

Jamie appeared from around the side of the house. "Hi Libby! Loving the outfit, but aren't you a bit nippy?"

"Ha ha, very funny," Libby replied. "I was enjoying a quiet swim when someone decided to join me."

"Oh no!" said Jamie, his eyes going wide. "I'm so sorry. I was unloading my van and figured he'd be alright running around back here. I didn't realise the door to the pool was open."

"Of course! It must have been left open, but that wasn't me. Seth came in after me."

Jamie raised his eyebrows. "You and Seth were taking an early morning dip together?"

Mortified, Libby tried to explain. "I thought I'd have the pool to myself, but then he came in, and left the door open so Barney ran in . . . and jumped right in!" she replied, trying not to blush.

"That's my afternoon taken up then," said Jamie with a sigh.

"I'm going to get inside and get properly dressed," said Libby, shivering.

"See you later. Sorry again," Jamie said.

* * *

Libby had a hot shower and some breakfast, before getting to work. Barney was also dry and seemed to be happy to curl up in his basket next to Libby's desk while she got started.

There were no emails from Seth so she started making her way through her list of jobs for the day, beginning with checking Seth's online calendar for the rest of the week to make sure she hadn't missed anything she needed to prepare for. She couldn't really risk upsetting her boss yet again. It was then she noticed Seth had added another appointment with herself for that afternoon. Oh god, these meetings had so far meant nothing good. Was he going to have another go at her about the stupid pool? Well, she wasn't going to let Jamie take the blame, she just wouldn't mention that he'd been watching Barney at the time. She imagined Seth would have forgotten that Jamie had been looking after the puppy by now anyway.

The rest of the morning dragged. Her stomach churned at the thought Seth was about to fire her: he wouldn't over a bit of mud and dog hair in his pool, would he? Surely not?

But he was really particular about how things were kept and not wasting time; having to have the pool cleaned out would definitely count as a waste of time, she feared . . .

Not feeling in the mood to chat, Libby stayed in her flat at lunch, just popping into the kitchen to make herself a quick sandwich. It wasn't nearly as much fun as having a chat with Sarah and she wished she'd stayed in the kitchen — maybe talking to Sarah would have taken her mind off things. Then she took Barney out into the garden so he'd wear himself out a bit and she could leave him in his crate while she had her meeting, which she knew wouldn't take long. No meeting with Seth ever took long.

She threw a tennis ball for the puppy and laughed at his antics as he chased after it like crazy, frequently falling over his own feet. If Seth did fire her, not only would she lose her job and her home, but she'd also never see Barney again. Who would look after him if she wasn't around? Jamie? But he didn't live on site. Maybe Seth would have him sent back to the breeder.

She picked the dog up and cuddled him, only releasing him when she realised the water from his wet paws was beginning to soak through her top — she'd have to change before she went up to see Seth in his office.

Finally, it was five to two, and Libby put Barney in his crate and put on a clean shirt. She grabbed a notepad and pen as she passed by her desk, really hoping he wanted to discuss something she'd need to take notes on and not just when she'd be receiving her final pay.

She drudged up the stairs to Seth's office, wanting the meeting to be over, but without having to attend it.

"Libby," Seth said, when she'd knocked and opened the door. "I wanted to speak to you about what happened this morning . . ."

"Okay . . ." replied Libby, not knowing what else to say. She really believed that she hadn't done anything wrong, but she also didn't want Jamie to take the blame for what had happened.

"I realise I left the door open to the pool building," Seth continued, "and that was how the puppy got it. Now I also understand you weren't responsible for the puppy at that point."

Libby went to open her mouth to say something, anything, in defence of Jamie, but Seth said, "I'm not angry with Jamie, don't worry. It never would have happened if I hadn't changed my plans. Poor Jamie's the one draining the pool this afternoon, so I think we can leave things at that."

"Right," said Libby, not quite believing she was getting away from the incident scot-free considering how angry Seth had been at the time.

"I also want to apologise for losing my temper," said Seth, uncomfortably. "It's not something I'm proud of, and it shouldn't have happened, especially as the incident had nothing to do with you. Though that's actually beside the point: I shouldn't have lost my temper at all."

"Thank you for saying that."

"I'm not sure if you've noticed, but I'm not very good when unexpected things pop up and I should have handled it a lot better. I'm also not very good with animals."

"Then why get a dog?" Libby asked bluntly, immediately regretting her outburst.

"Apparently having a pet, a dog in particular, is one of the things which makes us happiest in life. There have been several studies on it. I can email some over to you if you like . . ."

"But surely for the dog to make you happy, you need to spend some time with it, not just have it somewhere in the same, very large building as you."

"Well, yes."

Libby was on a roll now. "When are you going to spend some time with your dog exactly? Have you booked it into your diary yet?"

Seth's eyebrows shot up. Had she pushed him too far? Libby wondered. They were silent, weighing each other up.

"Book in whatever's necessary," Seth said finally, his eyes fixed on hers.

"He has a vet visit in an hour for his vaccinations. I can clear your schedule for you to take him," Libby suggested. She regretted it almost instantly. Seth didn't know Barney like she did, and he might be scared. "I could come as well," she added.

"Alright," Seth agreed. "I should come. As you very rightly point out, he's my dog. But I think he'll be calmer if you're there with him as well."

"Okay, we'll need to leave at three."

"We'll take your car," Seth said. "His crate's already in it."

Libby endeavoured to hide her disappointment. Once they'd finished at the vets', she'd hoped to get herself a nice coffee from a little cafe she liked near the river. Barney wouldn't be allowed around other dogs for another week, but he could sit on her lap and watch the world go by with her.

"Is everything alright?" Seth asked. Libby was surprised; it was unlike him to notice her expressions.

"Yes, everything's fine," she replied. "I'll see you later."

* * *

Barney's vaccinations went without a hitch. He was undoubtedly, in Libby's mind, the bravest puppy in the world. She and Seth had both taken pockets full of treats for him, and Seth had gone quite pale when they first took the puppy into the vet, but he seemed fine now the ordeal was over.

They walked out to the car and Libby put Barney in his crate.

"I can't believe there's a dog crate in the back of my Mercedes. That wasn't quite the look I was going for when I bought the car," commented Seth.

"What's supposed to make you happier; a crate-free, clean car, or a puppy?" Libby countered.

"The puppy, apparently," admitted Seth, sighing.

"And are your own findings consistent with those of the latest studies?" joked Libby.

"The jury's still out," Seth said, climbing into the passenger seat. "Vet visits are definitely not a positive experience."

"I would agree with you on that."

"Did you see the size of the needle they stuck in him? It was enormous!"

"It didn't seem to hurt him though," Libby reassured. "It certainly didn't stop him from eating the treats I was feeding him."

"That's true," said Seth, sounding reassured. "So he can go for proper walks in a week, the vet said?"

"He can hang out with other dogs in a week, but he can still only go for short walks. His joints can be damaged if he's walked too much when he's young."

"How do you know all this?"

"Google and YouTube videos," replied Libby honestly, making Seth laugh. His usually expressionless face seemed to come alive. She'd never seen him laugh before, and it made her smile.

* * *

As soon as Libby got back to her computer, she pulled up Seth's calendar. There really wasn't a lot of spare time in there — Seth was always either working, learning a skill, or exercising it seemed. Sundays were empty of any engagements when he was in the country, but were blocked out so Libby couldn't fill them in.

She did notice he took an hour for lunch every day — it seemed she'd have to hijack that.

* * *

At 1 p.m. the following afternoon, Libby once again knocked on the door to Seth's office, and once again heard him call out, "Come in!" The difference this time was that she was armed with tuna salad sandwiches and Barney, who had his lead on so he couldn't run in and cause havoc.

"Hello," said Seth, looking up from his computer screen.

"Hi," Libby replied. "You asked me to book you in some time with Barney, and this was the only slot available, so . . . here we are."

"Yes, I saw the change in my diary."

"Sarah sent lunch," Libby said, holding out the sandwiches.

Seth stood. "Okay . . . so what should I do with him?"

"He'd probably like a run around the garden. I've been working on getting him to come and sit. You could continue with that."

"Are you coming as well?"

"Um . . . I wasn't going to, but I can . . ."

"It would be helpful if you could show me what to do with him . . . Can you clear time to have your lunch break afterwards?"

"Sure," said Libby with a shrug. She'd never seen Seth look so uncertain of himself. His usual cool demeanour was rattled. She'd feel mean deserting him.

Libby carried Barney down the stairs — he still hadn't mastered them, and she wasn't keen on encouraging him to do so just yet.

She felt Seth watching her as she fussed over the puppy and put on her coat.

Once they were outside, Libby let Barney off the lead and he ran around, sniffing everything in sight.

Seth eyed the puppy cautiously. "So, what should I do with him?"

"I think he's happy exploring the garden at the moment. It's pretty big. Why don't we have our lunch while he plays and then we can do some training with him."

"Okay," said Seth.

They sat across from each other at the long table on the patio. Libby focused on eating her sandwich as quickly as possible. As soon as she was done they could start training Barney, which would at least mean they had something to talk about, instead of sitting in awkward silence as they were.

Eventually it just felt so awkward she had to break the stalemate, and commented, "Sarah makes lovely sandwiches."

"She does."

Silence resumed.

Finally, Libby swallowed the final bite of her food. "I'll run inside and grab Barney's treats and toys," she said, grateful to escape for a few minutes' respite. Seth was so difficult to talk to. She guessed it was because they had absolutely nothing in common, but it also didn't help that he always seemed to be watching and analysing her.

When she returned to the garden, Barney was with Seth and she was just in time to spot Seth giving the dog a bit of fish from his sandwich. "Don't do that!" she shouted out before she could stop herself. Both Seth and Barney jumped and turned towards her.

Libby's face reddened. She really must learn how to behave appropriately in front of her new boss.

"Sorry!" she said. "But if you feed him at the table, you'll never get rid of him."

As if to prove her point, Barney jumped up at Seth and put his front paws on his master's knees. Seth looked amused.

"Down, Barney," said Libby firmly, and gently took hold of the puppy's collar and removed him from Seth. "I know it's cute when he does stuff like that now, but he's going to be a big, strong dog. You can't have him jumping up at people, especially kids."

Seth gave her a contrite look. "You're right."

"And you're going to need to take him to puppy classes," continued Libby.

He laughed nervously. "Me?" Seth said.

"Yes, you. He's *your* dog," Libby said. "I love looking after him, I really do, he's so sweet, but he is your dog." She waited for Seth's reaction. She didn't want to overstep the line with her boss, but she also couldn't keep doing everything for Barney. Yes, things would get easier with him as he got older, she knew, but he would still be a major distraction when she was trying to work.

"If he's too much for you to handle, I can organise for a dogsitter, or for Jamie to help more," Seth said.

Libby couldn't help rolling her eyes. "But what's the point in having a dog if you're not going to spend any time with him? It's certainly not going to prove any of the studies you've read about dogs improving your life."

"I'm very busy."

"I know you are," she said, raising an eyebrow. "I see your schedule."

"So, what do you suggest?"

"A walk or training every lunchtime, and a longer walk on Sundays once Barney's had his vaccinations."

"I can't do Sundays," Seth said, firmly. "But when he's bigger he can come on runs with me, and we'll work on him being in my office sometimes."

"Deal," said Libby, holding out her hand. Seth shook it, a flicker of amusement playing on his face.

"It would probably be a good idea to enrol him in some kind of puppy class. Can you begin researching them asap?" Seth asked. "Book him in for whatever looks best, and pop it in my diary."

"You'll be coming then?" questioned Libby.

"Yes. As you like to remind me, he's my dog," said Seth. "We can also start getting him to sleep in the kitchen overnight."

"That's alright," said Libby, quickly. "He can stay with me at night."

"Are you sure?"

"Yes," Libby said. "I'm used to having him in my room now, I'd miss him."

"Okay." Seth was quiet, fiddling with one of the balls Libby had brought outside for the puppy. "Thanks for calling me out on this," he said.

"No problem," said Libby, with a shrug.

"Right, what shall we do with this puppy then?" Seth asked, standing up. "Don't worry about taking your own notes. I'll get it all down on my phone."

"You're going to take notes?"

"Yes, of course," said Seth. "How else are we going to be able to tell how quickly he's grasping things and whether there's anything we need to particularly work on?"

"I think if he's incapable of sitting when asked to in a couple of months' time, we'll figure we're doing something wrong."

Seth's look told Libby he wasn't prepared to leave anything up to chance.

"And I need to record how he's affecting me," Seth added. Oh yeah, Libby had forgotten that the puppy was a research project for a while there.

Returning to her desk at the end of their hour with Barney, Libby was proud of herself for speaking her mind to Seth. He was still a complete nightmare, but at least she knew he was willing to listen to her and to bend a little when necessary.

Barney curled up in his basket and fell fast asleep within seconds.

Libby was pulled from an Instagram post she was writing by her mobile ringing. "Hi Mel," Libby answered. "How are you?"

"I'm good, thanks, sweetie! I was calling to check up on how you were settling in. Do you need me to look around for something else, or are you going to stay for a while, do you think?"

"It's definitely been different," admitted Libby, looking down at Barney. "But it's getting better, I think. Keep me in mind if anything really interesting turns up though." She didn't want to burn her bridges.

"Honey, we're a temp office! You've got the most interesting job that's come into this office in years,"

"Fair enough," said Libby, laughing.

"Why don't you use this time to work out what you actually want to do?" her friend suggested.

"I know, I should. I'm just not sure where to start. I mean, how did you know you wanted to run a temp agency?"

"I like people and helping them. I guess I'm organised and a bit bossy, so it seemed like a good fit."

"You make it sound so easy."

"Sorry."

"Don't be!" Libby laughed. "It's not your fault I can't manage to get my life together."

"You are doing brilliantly!" said her friend immediately. "You dealt with what Robert did amazingly, and now look at you with a new job and a fantastic new flat."

"Thanks to you."

"Nope. Apparently your new boss is notoriously hard to please, yet he sent me a glowing report on your first couple of weeks."

"Really?" Libby asked, stunned.

"Yes! He said you're capable and creative."

"Seriously? I cannot imagine Seth writing that."

"He did, and I wasn't at all surprised."

"Well! Thanks, Melissa."

"I'll speak to you soon."

"Okay, bye."

That was a shock, Libby thought. Apart from mentioning that he'd liked her photos once, she'd had no real feedback from Seth. She felt a little warm glow now she knew he didn't think she was completely useless.

* * *

On Friday evening Libby was cooking herself a huge, extremely spicy vegetable curry. She left it bubbling away on the hob while she went to give her flat a tidy. She'd had a surprisingly great couple of days. She was still a little in shock that she'd been so bold as to tell Seth he had to spend time with Barney, and that he'd agreed and had gone to the vet with her. She hadn't been looking forward to taking Barney, but he'd been fine. And Seth had begun training Barney and had committed to walking him. She couldn't help wondering if the puppy would make her boss happier, or at least more relaxed.

She'd even ended up enjoying a conversation with Seth while they'd trained Barney the day before. They'd chatted about photography and Seth told her about an exhibition he'd been to in New York. When he switched off from work, he was good company.

She picked up Barney's toys that lay strewn about her sitting room and grinned at the sight of the tiny bright pink Christmas tree she'd treated herself to, and put on a table, out of Barney's reach. She usually decorated on the first day of December without fail, but she'd been so busy this year, it had slipped her mind. Or maybe she'd been subconsciously trying not to think about the festive season because of not spending it being with Robert as she'd planned. But she'd always loved decorating the Christmas tree; it made her happy.

She took a sip from the glass of Chablis she'd brought through with her and sang along to her favourite singer-songwriter playlist on Spotify. She was pleased it was the weekend and was looking forward to a Netflix marathon (another benefit of living in Seth's house was that he appeared to have every television subscription service going). Maybe she'd also take Barney to meet Melissa tomorrow. Though, she reminded herself, she wouldn't be able to stay for long though because Melissa didn't have a garden to let Barney out in.

Libby was so engrossed in her singing and weekend planning, that she jumped when Barney began barking. It was only when she turned to check why Barney had gone running over to the French windows that she spotted her boss.

She wiped her hands on a tea towel and went to let him in. Barney, thrilled to see Seth, jumped around like he hadn't seen him for years rather than just a couple of hours.

"Sorry to disturb you. Nice . . . um . . . tree," he said, quickly as he fussed over the puppy. "I tried knocking at your office door . . ."

"The music," explained Libby, unnecessarily.

"Yes. Anyway, I was thinking of taking Barney out with me on Sunday and I wanted to check you hadn't got anything planned with him."

"Um, no. Nothing planned."

"Great, I'll come and get him at eleven."

"I thought you said you couldn't do anything with Barney on Sundays?"

"I changed my mind," said Seth, simply. "Don't worry, I won't take him anywhere where other dogs have been."

"Great," Libby replied.

She was desperate to know where Seth was taking Barney. Where did her employer go and what did he do every Sunday? But it definitely wasn't her place to ask.

Barney brought a ball over to Seth.

"Sorry, Barney, I've got to go and let Libby get back to her evening — whatever you're cooking smells amazing, by the way."

"Thanks. My culinary skills are nothing compared to Sarah's but I do make a mean curry. I spent part of my gap year in Sri Lanka and did a cookery course there."

"Wow," replied Seth.

"Would you like to stay and have some?" Libby somehow found herself asking.

"I've got a date, otherwise I'd love to," replied Seth rather formally, making Libby cringe with embarrassment at him letting her down so gently. She had no idea why the stupid idea had even popped into her head. She must have been overexcited at the fact that they managed to spend some time together where she didn't do anything stupid, and when Seth wasn't cross with her. Anyway, she was having a great evening, she didn't want to spend it with her boss, and she was certain he wouldn't want to spend it with her.

"Have a nice time," Libby said, and was relieved when Seth replied, "You too, I'll see you tomorrow."

Somehow her evening had now been disturbed though, and she found she couldn't recapture the relaxed feel of it. She caught herself thinking about Seth's date. What sort of woman was he attracted to, she wondered.

She heard his car start and drive away, so he wasn't having supper with his date in the house. Would he bring her back later? And why was she even wasting her head space with these things?

She ended up going to bed earlier than planned but was still awake when Seth returned, alone from what she could make out, as her ears strained to pick up voices or footsteps.

CHAPTER 7

As much as Libby wanted to spend her puppy-free hours on Sunday doing something fun, she knew it was the perfect opportunity to collect the rest of her stuff from Robert's flat — it was his dad's birthday, so he'd be visiting his parents.

She still had her key, but wouldn't feel right letting herself into the home that wasn't hers anymore without checking it was alright with Robert first, so she texted him: *Hi, is it okay for me to pick up my things Sunday afternoon? I can let myself in and post keys through the letterbox.*

She didn't need to wait long for a reply: *Sure. I won't be in.*

Part of Libby breathed a sigh of relief that she knew she wouldn't have to see Robert — the way she was still feeling, she never wanted to see that cheating scumbag again — but she was also hurt he didn't seem to miss her and had moved on with his life so easily. Maybe he was still seeing the woman she'd caught him with. Maybe she'd even moved in with him . . . But surely even Robert would be kind enough to warn her if that was the case. And he hadn't said "*we* won't be in".

* * *

Seth knocked on the French doors at exactly eleven on Sunday as Libby knew he would and caused Barney to go wild with excitement.

"What's with all the boxes?" he asked, spotting the pile of banana crates she'd picked up from the supermarket the night before.

"I'm picking up my stuff from my old house this afternoon," Libby replied as breezily as she could.

"It was nice of your old flatmates to store it for you until now," Seth commented.

"Old boyfriend, actually."

"Oh."

"Yeah, it's all a bit awkward. I'll be glad to have everything out of there."

"Have you got someone to give you a hand?"

"No, I'll be fine on my own. Robert, my ex, isn't going to be there and there isn't that much for me to pack up. It should all fit in the Mercedes. Anyway, here's Barney's lead. Shall we go and move his crate into your car?"

"Okay, sure," Seth replied, then paused, like he wanted to say something else. He apparently decided against it though as he put the lead on the puppy, accepted a handful of poo bags, and followed Libby to the front of the house where their cars were parked.

The crate was swiftly put in Seth's car and he drove off with Barney, leaving Libby still curious to know where the two of them were going.

* * *

Libby put off leaving for Robert's house for as long as she could, convincing herself she needed to clean and tidy her new flat before she left, but eventually, she managed to drive over. Despite knowing he wasn't going to be home, she was relieved that Robert's car was nowhere to be seen and, summoning her courage, let herself into the house.

Everything looked exactly the same as when she'd lived there, and a quick glance around didn't yield any evidence of another woman having moved in. No Christmas decorations had been put up yet, she noticed. She began work downstairs, leaving Robert the majority of their joint things, only packing anything she had an emotional attachment to. She was surprised by how quickly the car filled up; she'd underestimated how much space her things would need. It looked like she'd have to make a second trip if she didn't have time to take a load back to Seth's, unload it all and then come back and load the car up again that day. Oh well, she thought, she'd just have to see how much she could get done.

She tried not to get bogged down in memories as she packed, focusing on getting the task done as quickly as possible, but when she heard a knock at the door, despite knowing it wouldn't be Robert, her stomach did a little nervous jump.

Opening the door, she found herself facing Seth with Barney in his arms. The puppy wriggled, his tail going crazy, as he attempted to get to Libby.

"Hi," Libby said, blankly. "Um . . . what are you doing here?"

"Well, um . . . can I put him down in the house?" Seth asked.

"Okay." She stood aside, confused.

Barney was put down and promptly began sniffing everything in the hallway.

"I thought you might need a hand with your stuff," Seth explained, looking a little embarrassed. "The Mercedes isn't huge, and your boxes might be heavy . . ."

"Thanks, that's nice of you," said Libby, trying to keep the surprise out of her voice. "How did you know where I'd be?"

"You filled in your last address on one of the forms when you came to work for me. I looked it up on my phone."

"I thought you were busy on Sundays."

"I am. I finished early."

"Well . . . In that case, I would love some help. There definitely isn't enough space for everything in my car. I was worried I'd have to come back again next week."

"Just tell me what you need me to carry."

Libby handed him a full banana crate and they set to work in surprisingly companionable silence.

* * *

An hour later, Libby straightened up from her last box. "I think that's everything," she said.

"Do you want to do one last scan of the place before we leave?"

"No, I'd rather go. It's getting late and I don't want to bump into my ex when he gets back."

Seth hesitated. "I take it that things didn't end well between you."

"You could say that." Libby debated going into more detail about what had happened between her and Robert, but it was personal, and Seth was her boss, so it probably wasn't appropriate.

"Oh no," Seth said. He pointed to a large stain on the carpet. A very guilty-looking Barney stood next to it. "I'm sorry, I should have been keeping a closer eye on the time. It's been a while since he last had a chance to pee."

"Don't worry. To be honest, I think it's a perfect leaving present," said Libby with a laugh. "We'd probably better let him out in the back garden before he gets in the car though."

Libby took Barney into the little postage-stamp sized yard while Seth carried the last couple of banana crates out to the car. Libby gave a final glance at the house she and Robert had shared: she knew she was well out of it, and she was so lucky to have the home she did now, but that didn't stop the memories from consuming her.

Shaking her head, Libby locked the door behind her, posted the house keys through the letter box and gave Seth a thumbs up before getting in the Mercedes and following him back to St George's Hill.

* * *

83

"Thank you again for coming to help me," Libby said once they finished unpacking both cars and all her stuff was in her little flat. "It made all the difference."

"Not a problem, I was happy to help."

"We'd better give Barney his tea now, it's a bit overdue."

"Show me how to do it," said Seth. "I should know what to feed him."

"Sure," Libby replied. "I usually give him breakfast in here and most of his other meals in your kitchen, so there's a food supply in both places."

"Let's go to my kitchen then so I can see where everything's kept."

They walked through to the main house, Barney close at their heels — he definitely knew they were on their way to get him his dinner. He ran ahead of them to the cupboard containing his food, his tail wagging like crazy.

"Are you excited, buddy?" asked Seth, smiling.

"Apparently all retrievers are food obsessed," said Libby.

"And he's certainly no exception."

"So he has two scoops of the food from this bag," Libby explained. She put the food in the bowl and put the bowl on the floor. "And he knows he has to wait until he's told he can have it."

Barney sat gazing from the bowl of food to Libby and back again.

"Okay!" Libby said, and Barney leapt on his supper. He finished it in about thirty seconds flat.

"Wow, that was . . . impressive."

Libby laughed. "Yeah, he doesn't hang around."

"Would you like a glass of wine?" Seth asked. "To celebrate you being properly moved in," he added.

"Um . . . sure, thank you," said Libby. It was a big deal that she'd moved everything out from what she was now firmly referring to as 'Robert's house'. She deserved to celebrate.

"I'll be back in a minute," Seth said. Libby heard him going down the stairs to the cellar. She absentmindedly checked her phone; there was nothing from Robert. Perhaps he wasn't back from his parents' house yet . . . What did it matter anyway? Maybe he was cross about the pee. Well, he more than deserved it. Should she send him a quick text to check he'd got the keys okay? She began typing but was interrupted by Seth returning with a bottle of wine.

"I think you'll like this," he said, holding up a bottle of red wine for her to see. Libby knew next to nothing about wine, her method of choosing was to go with whatever bottle was six quid or under in the supermarket and had the most money off, but it was kind of him to pick out something special for her.

"Thanks," Libby said, accepting a large glass. She took a sip. "Oh wow, this is absolutely delicious," she said, honestly. It was soft and fruity, and she could tell the difference between that and what she usually drank.

"I'm glad you like it. It's from a little vineyard I visited in Napa Valley last year while I was doing a wine-tasting course."

"I love California," said Libby, "but I've never been to Napa Valley. I haven't been further north than San Francisco."

"It's beautiful. I spent a lot of my time there gazing out at sunsets with a glass of wine in my hand rather than actually learning anything." He shook his head ruefully.

Libby laughed. "It sounds like you enjoyed yourself anyway."

As they drank the wine, Libby couldn't help but wonder about the change in Seth. This couldn't be the same uptight boss she'd been dealing with for the last few weeks. Then she noticed they were leaning toward each other, their bodies mirroring, seemingly at the same time as Seth did.

He shifted back, a frown appearing on his forehead, and said, "Why don't you take Barney outside and I'll scrape together some food for us from the fridge."

"Okay," Libby said, automatically. Had she agreed to have supper with him? How had this happened? Then again, it wasn't like she had anything else planned, and she definitely wasn't in the mood to cook.

"Come on then, Barney," she called. The puppy got up and followed her outside onto the patio. Libby wrapped her arms around her and looked up at the stars while Barney ran around, sniffing and examining goodness only knows what. She closed her eyes. It had been a tiring afternoon, physically and emotionally.

"Here we go," she heard Seth call. She opened her eyes and called the puppy before going back into the kitchen.

"Hang on, there's more," Seth said, his head inside the huge American-style fridge freezer.

Seth had laid out a wooden board on the table covered in cheeses, salami, ham, grapes, olives and hummus. Libby's stomach rumbled at the sight of it.

"Shall we eat in here?" Seth asked, cutting up a loaf of ciabatta.

"That's fine with me," Libby replied. "Can I get anything?"

"Some knives and a plate each would be great," Seth said, as he put the bread in a bowl.

"You've created a feast!" said Libby, laughing.

Seth refilled their glasses. "I may have gone a bit over the top," he admitted, "but I'm really hungry."

"Me too," Libby said, placing plates in front of them and helping herself to some bread.

Seth sliced salami for them and handed some to Libby.

"Are you glad to be all moved out of your ex-boyfriend's place?"

"*So* glad," said Libby. "He . . . cheated on me."

"He's an idiot," said Seth firmly."

Libby smiled, "Thank you. How was your date the other night?" she dared to ask.

Seth took a moment to answer, and Libby worried she'd overstepped the mark, but he finally replied, "Awkward, to be honest. A friend of mine thought it would be a good idea to set me up. It wasn't."

"That's a shame," Libby commented, ignoring the fact that her mood had gone up a huge notch.

Seth shrugged in response.

Barney was tired out from his busy day. He settled down by Libby's feet and fell asleep, snoring quietly.

"Did Barney behave himself for you before you joined me?" asked Libby, remembering she'd forgotten to ask before.

"He was really good," Seth said. "He was outside most of the time, so I didn't need to worry about accidents. Oh, he did try to chase a cat though. I don't think he'll do it again. He received a thump on his nose."

Libby laughed. "Poor Barney, I'm sure he was only trying to be friendly."

So Seth had taken Barney somewhere with a garden and a cat — what did he get up to on Sundays? She knew it was none of her business, and she'd hate it if Seth was nosing around in her private life, but she couldn't help being intrigued and wondering how she could go about solving this mystery.

CHAPTER 8

Libby and Sarah were taking their coffee break together the following morning, when Seth surprised them by breezing in. "So, today's the big day," he said.

Sarah recovered first. "Big day?"

"Barney's finally allowed to go for his first proper walk today. And his first puppy class is at six," Libby explained.

"Did you have plans to take him anywhere for his walk?" Seth asked. "Only, I thought we could go somewhere together . . . as it's the first one."

"Oh. Sure," said Libby, surprised. Part of her still worried Seth saw Barney as a bit of a science experiment, especially as he continued to take notes both during training sessions and when he was supposedly relaxing with the dog.

"Great. Sarah, do you think you could fix us some lunch to take with us, please?" Seth asked.

"Absolutely," said Sarah, who appeared to be struggling to hide a smile.

"Libby, have you got time to look up somewhere nice we can take him? He can't walk for very long at a time though . . . But maybe we could stop and let him have a break while we eat?"

"There's a little river walk nearby I think he'd like. There should be lots of other dogs there for him to be introduced to, and there are benches for us to sit and have our lunch at."

"Sounds good. I'll meet you by your car at one," said Seth. Picking up the bulletproof coffee Sarah had automatically made him, he left to get back to work.

"I guess that's my cue to finish my break," said Libby, smiling at Sarah.

"See you later," said Sarah. "Enjoy your walk together. Should I pack some champagne?"

"Don't be daft!" said Libby. "I'm just trying to get him to take an interest in his dog, which hasn't been easy."

"He seems great with Barney now. I mean Barney did follow him out of here," Sarah teased.

"Which goes to show that what I'm doing is working."

"Whatever you say," said Sarah cryptically.

* * *

A couple of hours later, Libby, Seth and Barney arrived at the little car park at the start of the riverside walk. She slotted the Mercedes neatly into a space, and while Seth got himself a double espresso and Libby a latte from the cafe, Libby put Barney's lead on and got him out of the car making sure her pockets were full of treats and dog poo bags.

"Come on, Barney!" said Libby cheerfully, and they set off down the footpath.

It was cold and cloudy, but the rain seemed to be holding off, and Libby enjoyed feeling the chill on her cheeks, glad she'd remembered to bring a hat and scarf.

Barney seemed nervous of some of the larger dogs coming over to greet him, but with some encouragement, he was soon making friends.

"Shall we let him off the lead?" Seth asked.

"I don't know . . ." Libby said, uncertainly. Looking around, she could see about a million dangers for a small puppy.

"He's been doing well with his recall," said Seth. "And most of the other dogs are off-lead."

It was clear Seth thought Barney should be let off and, after all, he was Seth's dog so Libby didn't feel she could argue the point with him, even if she didn't think it was a good idea.

"Okay," she said, "But we should probably put him back on for the way back in case he runs off into the car park."

"Sure," said Seth. He unclipped the lead. It took Barney a second to realise what had happened. As soon as he did, he began to run around, thrilled at his new-found freedom to explore all the wonderful smells around him. He wandered back and forth, sniffing everything, his tail wagging crazily. Then he stopped and stared at something. Libby followed his gaze: there was a squirrel in the middle of the grass about ten metres away from the puppy. Libby opened her mouth to suggest to Seth that he put Barney back on the lead, but before she managed to utter a word, Barney bolted.

Libby's heart felt like it had flown into her mouth. Should she run after Barney? Or would he think that was some kind of game?

"Barney!" called Seth firmly from next to her. "Come!"

His commanding voice sent a pleasant shiver down Libby's spine. *What was going on with her?* she wondered, shaking her head.

Barney stopped, contemplating the squirrel for a moment before looking back at his master. Libby held her breath. Barney gave a final bark at the squirrel and came running back to them.

"Good boy!" Seth said, giving Barney a treat and a stroke on the ears before reattaching his lead. Libby could see by the look of relief on his face that Seth had been nearly as worried as she had been.

"I think maybe that's enough time off the lead for him today," said Seth, sheepishly.

"I agree."

They continued on their walk, letting Barney decide the direction they went in, and stopped to eat their lunch quickly before heading back to the car.

"That could definitely have gone worse," commented Seth.

"I think he did really well, considering it was his first time," said Libby, much happier now that Barney was firmly back on his lead.

Libby took the opportunity to take some photos of Barney and Seth as they walked. There was a particularly sweet moment when Seth picked the puppy up and was given a firm lick on his nose, which she managed to catch perfectly. She went through them when they were home and was pleased — in fact, she'd say they were some of her best work. On a whim, she attached the best five to an email and sent them to Seth.

* * *

Libby was called into Seth's office later that day.

"The photos you sent me . . ." he said as soon as she came in.

"I thought they might be useful if you end up writing something about the whole 'dogs making you happy' thing?" Libby said. "Just delete them if you don't like them. They were only snaps I took quickly . . ."

"They're really good — maybe even better than the other pictures you've done for me. Have you thought about doing photography professionally?"

"Well, I'd possibly like to, but it's never really been an option . . ."

"There are loads of courses available . . ."

"I'm sure there are," said Libby, not wanting to admit that photography had always been too expensive for her to be able to take seriously. "Anyway, I'll let you get back to work. I've got to finish going through that blog post before putting it live at five."

"Okay, thanks again."

"And the puppy class is at six this evening," Libby reminded him. "We'll need to leave by twenty to."

"No problem," Seth said, not looking up from his laptop.

"And you're sure you want to come?"

"Yep. I'll meet you and Barney at your car later."

* * *

True to his word, Seth was ready and waiting for Libby when she emerged, slightly flustered, from the house at quarter to six.

"You're late," he snapped.

"Sorry, Barney had a bit of an incident," replied Libby.

"We're going to miss the beginning of the class."

"We'll be even later if we stand around arguing," commented Libby as she put Barney into the car.

Amazingly, Seth got in the car without any further complaints, but Libby decided not to push her luck by attempting to chat with him.

They pulled into the car park of the community centre where Libby did her yoga.

"The class will have already started," Seth muttered grumpily while Libby got Barney out of the car.

"If you grab my bag for me, we'll be faster," Libby said through gritted teeth.

Seth marched to the door of the centre and pulled it open. "Hang on!" called Libby, who was tangled in the puppy's lead. "Barney should have a pee before we go in."

Seth let out an exasperated sigh.

Barney did his business and he and Libby rejoined Seth. "You do understand that nothing terrible happens if you're five minutes late for a puppy class, don't you?" Libby asked Seth.

"It's the principle," he snapped back.

Libby decided to ignore this.

They went through the doors of the building and along a corridor to the hall which had seven other puppies and their owners already milling about in it.

"Are you sure this is the best class available?" Seth whispered.

"Yes!" hissed back Libby. "The teacher goes to my yoga class!"

"How does that make her qualified to train puppies?" Seth retorted. Libby elbowed him, gesturing to the small woman in her sixties who was heading towards them, clipboard in hand. She wore jeans and a fleece jumper and a baseball cap on her grey hair.

"We apologise for being late," Seth said.

"Don't worry!" she responded cheerfully. "We haven't started yet! Lovely to see you here, Libby!"

Libby threw Seth a told-you-so look which he ignored.

"Okay, everyone!" said the lady with the clipboard. "My name's Judith and I'm going to be taking this class, and this is my dog, Meggie." She stroked the head of a very relaxed-looking Irish setter. "Let's all sit in a semi-circle," she continued. "If you could all please keep your puppies on their leads, to begin with. There'll be plenty of time for them to socialise in just a little while."

Seth did not look impressed as he sat down, brushing the floor beneath him surreptitiously as he did so.

The next hour flew by for Libby. Barney may not have performed everything he was asked to perfectly, but he came when he was called most of the time, and sat when instructed. He was also one of the few puppies who didn't have an accident during the session, for which a bottle of cleaning fluid and some kitchen roll were provided in the corner.

And it was sweet to see how much Barney loved playing with the other puppies, especially a Springer Spaniel called Dennis, who he chased all around the hall.

When the class ended and everyone began to collect up their dogs, Judith came over to Libby and Seth. "I hope you've enjoyed your first class," she said. "Barney did very well."

Libby could practically feel herself glowing with pride. Judith continued: "We have lots of other groups going on as well. All the details are on this, or I'm sure Libby will fill you in." She handed Seth a leaflet.

"Thank you," said Seth. Libby stifled a giggle at the thought of Seth join the weekly bridge group.

"We're trying to raise as many funds as possible," Judith explained. "There's a large part of the roof at the back of the building that needs replacing, and there's been talk of the building being sold if it's not sorted out soon. Obviously, this would be terrible for the local community, so many people rely on this centre."

Seth's phone rang. He scowled at the screen and signalled to Libby and Judith that he needed to take the call. While she waited for Seth, Libby attached Barney's lead to his harness and chatted with some of the other dog owners.

She looked over to see if Seth was almost done, just in time to see a little dalmatian pup cock his leg and pee all over Seth's trousers. She hid her smile. Oops! All in all, a most satisfying evening.

CHAPTER 9

Libby was surprised to see a large portion of the afternoon blocked off for both her and Seth when she logged into her computer the following morning. She questioned him about it during what she now thought of as 'Barney Time'.

"I need your help with a project I'm working on," Seth said cryptically. "I think you'll enjoy it."

Seeing that Libby was going to question him further, he said. "Meet me in the gym at two thirty and all shall be revealed. Oh, and make sure you wear something comfortable that you can move around in."

Libby was intrigued. One of the things she hadn't expected with Seth was how unpredictable he was, especially as he seemed so regimented: she honestly never knew what he was going to suggest she do next. It certainly made a change from living with Robert, a man who never knowingly did anything unexpected. Until he decided to sleep with another woman, that is.

Five minutes before she was due to meet Seth she tied her hair back into a ponytail and changed into a t-shirt and jogging bottoms — she may not look glamorous, but if there was one thing she'd learnt since beginning working with Seth, the man who lived in jeans and t-shirts, it was that if

he told you to dress in comfortable clothes, you really ought
to dress in comfortable clothes.

* * *

Libby had never been in Seth's gym before. Despite her best
intentions to make the most of everything at her disposal,
the space had seemed intimidating, with all the machines
lined up in rows she could see through the huge windows.
The room she found Seth in was separate from the main gym
and seemed to be a dance studio as far as she could tell from
the mirror and barre along one side. There were no windows,
which Libby was grateful for; she dreaded the thought of
Jamie or Sarah watching her doing whatever it was that Seth
had planned for her. How exactly did she get herself into
these situations?

Seth was wearing his gym gear and was standing next
to a CD player.

"What's going on, Coleman?" asked Libby, her hands
on her hips.

"We're learning to waltz," said Seth. "It's the skill I've
set myself to master for the next few months."

A woman came in behind Libby. She was tall and very,
very slim. Her hair was up in a tight bun and she wore black
leggings and a loose, sleeveless black top. She looked in her
early fifties but could have been older.

"Libby, meet Madame Blanchet who has kindly agreed
to teach us to waltz."

"I . . . wasn't aware that I wanted to learn to waltz,"
replied Libby.

"If you look in your contract," countered Seth, "you'll be
aware that this job is a little unusual and sometimes involves
learning new skills."

"To be honest, I'm most surprised that you own what
can only be termed as a 'boom box' — are we back in 1990?"
said Libby, pointing at the machine in the corner of the room.

"I haven't got reliable Wi-Fi in here yet, and Madame Blanchet had a particular CD she wants us to work from," responded Seth, a smile tugging at the corners of his mouth.

Madame Blanchet clapped her hands sharply. "Now, now you two, stop your flirting! We have work to do," she said firmly.

Both Seth and Libby snapped round to face her. "We're not flirting," they said together. They glared at one another.

Madame Blanchet shrugged. "Whatever it is you're doing, it is time to stop and concentrate on your lesson."

She beckoned to them to stand together and placed Libby's hand on Seth's shoulder and Seth's hand on Libby's waist. She walked smoothly over to the CD player and pressed play.

"Seth has already learnt the basics from me last week. Have you danced before, Libby?" she asked.

"Only after a decent drink," replied Libby, stifling her giggles at the crazy situation she currently found herself in. Madame Blanchet glared at her.

"The waltz is very romantic and very simple. You must be close," she said firmly, pushing Seth and Libby's bodies together. Libby felt a tingle run through her and jolted back with surprise. Madame Blanchet moved her back into position. Seth's face remained impassive, appearing not to have felt anything.

"The key to a successful waltz is timing and staying together. Watch," said Madame Blanchet. She held out her arms and began waltzing elegantly around the studio, head held high and back ramrod straight. She chanted, "1, 2, 3," Libby did her best to study what the teacher's feet were doing, but it was hard when all her body wanted to do was focus on how close Seth was.

He smelled of sandalwood, presumably from whatever shampoo or shower gel he'd used that morning. The smell made Libby feel slightly faint, but she couldn't stop herself from sniffing as surreptitiously as possible.

"Libby, you must just follow Seth on his lead. He will show you what to do. Ready . . . and go!"

Before she knew it, Libby was being dragged around the dance floor by a very focused-looking Seth. He counted quietly under his breath. He stood stiffly and stared straight ahead over Libby's head. Libby, by contrast, spent the first dance attempting to keep time and trying to work out where on earth her feet were supposed to go. She didn't think she was doing too badly, considering she'd never done any ballroom dancing before in her life — though she did step on Seth's toes a few times.

* * *

Finally, the music stopped and so did their dancing. Libby looked up and her eyes met Seth's. He let go of her, not realising the extent he'd been supporting her, and she stumbled slightly. He caught her gently. "Are you alright?" he asked.

"I'm just a little . . . dizzy."

Their eyes met again.

The heat from Seth's body seemed to radiate through Libby and every molecule of her being was acutely aware of how close she was to him.

"No, no, this won't do!" snapped Madame Blanchet.

Seth let go of Libby again, but slowly this time. Dare she believe he did so reluctantly? What was going on here?

"You are bent like a question mark!" Madame Blanchet continued, directing her disapproval at Libby. "And why are you so fixated on your feet? Yet I do not believe you stepped once in time to the music. I would not have thought it possible!"

"I never claimed to be a dancer!" countered Libby. "If Seth had informed me what we were going to be doing, I would have told him that!"

"You will need extra sessions," Madame Blanchet declared. "Can this be arranged? I have some beginner classes which may help."

"That's not a problem," said Seth. "Libby, if you can liaise with Madame and take whatever classes she deems necessary. Have them charged to my account."

Something in Libby snapped. "No," she said firmly.

"No, what?" asked Seth.

"I have no desire to learn ballroom dancing, Seth, and as Madame Blanchet has very eloquently pointed out, I'm no good at it. I also do not have time to do all my personal assistant duties, look after a puppy, and practise with you every day, as you will no doubt expect me to do, as well as taking additional dance classes. It isn't going to happen."

Seth looked momentarily shocked, but then a small smile appeared on his face. "Fair enough," he said. "I should have asked you if you had the time first, but I wasn't sure you would have agreed to come and try it out."

"You're right, I wouldn't," admitted Libby. "And I think the past quarter of an hour has shown you why."

"Madame Blanchet," Seth said, "would you please be able to organise a new dance partner for me?"

Madame Blanchet nodded. Libby could swear the woman looked relieved.

"Can I go now?" asked Libby.

"Sure. At least my toes will be grateful," said Seth, mock grimacing.

Libby left as quickly as she could, amazed she'd been able to extricate herself so easily. Who knows, she might have ended up enjoying ballroom dancing, maybe even become passable if not actually good at it. But her head was screaming at her that being that close to Seth Coleman, and the feelings it produced, was definitely not a good idea.

* * *

Libby was proud of herself for standing up to Seth until the gate buzzer went the next afternoon, heralding the arrival of Seth's new dance partner.

The dancer parked her ancient-looking red Fiat Panda in front of the house and stepped out of it. She was beautiful, statuesque, slim and blonde, she looked like she'd stepped out of a dancewear catalogue. The young dancer even walked beautifully. *That's what natural grace looks like*, thought Libby with just a touch of bitterness.

Libby felt a tendril of jealousy reaching up inside her. What was going on? Sure, Seth was good-looking, there was no denying that. He *was* very fit and muscular . . .

Yet the fact remained that he was her boss, and she couldn't do anything to jeopardise her job and home. Well, anything other than constantly embarrassing herself in front of him and disagreeing with most things he suggested . . . frankly, it was amazing he was still employing her.

* * *

Libby had to wait until Barney Time the next day to subtly quiz Seth about his new dance partner.

"So," she said, as they sat down with some delicious, filled flatbread Sarah had made for lunch, "you found your new dance partner quickly."

"Yes," was the only reply she received.

"What's her name?" Libby probed.

"Saskia," Seth replied. "She's a student at Madame Blanchet's school."

"Was she any good?"

"Yeah, my toes aren't as sore as when I danced with you anyway," Seth teased.

"Oi," Libby said, giving him a gentle push. "Was I that bad?"

"Yes," said Seth honestly. "But you would have improved."

"So, you're going to stick with her then?" asked Libby.

"Yes, I think so," said Seth, finishing off his food. "Right, Barney, let's see if we can get you to bring me your toy more than one time in ten, eh?"

Libby watched Seth play with his dog. She didn't need to be here with them anymore. Seth was bonding well with Barney and was more than capable of looking after him for an hour, which would give her a break from the puppy. But, she realised, Barney Time had become her favourite time of the day. Of course, it helped that the weather had been kind, and she doubted she'd feel quite so keen if she was eating her lunch outside without the patio heaters on . . .

But then the allure of Barney Time wasn't just the opportunity to be outside and away from her desk for an hour, nor was it playing with Barney himself, as cute as he was. The simple fact of the matter was that Libby enjoyed Seth's company. He knew a lot about a lot of different topics which made him interesting to talk to, and she liked seeing him interacting with the puppy. She was very aware that there was a line between them, a very important line, the line between employer and employee, but that didn't mean that she couldn't enjoy spending time with him, did it?

* * *

Seth was away for a couple of days at a conference in Norwich and Libby wasn't needed so she stayed at the house with Barney which suited her fine. Her workload was less as she didn't have to prepare anything for any Zoom or in-person meetings Seth might have, so she was able to go to Annie's yoga class most days while Jamie watched Barney, and spend some more time on photography, either for Seth's website or, after work hours, for her own pleasure.

The weather was crisp and sunny, leaving a frost on the lawn which gradually cleared as the morning went on. So, Libby managed to get outside early to catch the light on the ice and focused on nature photography, something she hadn't properly worked on before starting work for Seth. Barney wasn't very patient and tended to use any opportunity she tried to take to set up a photo to wind his lead around her legs or start to eat something he shouldn't. He was very cute though, so she found she couldn't be cross.

Strangely it was during the evenings that Libby missed Seth the most. There was something about knowing the rest of the house was empty, even when she didn't usually see the other occupant, that made her feel a bit lonely. Barney also seemed to be missing his master. Libby kept catching him slinking off to go and search Seth's office.

* * *

Libby had just returned to work when she heard Seth's car stop outside the house. Her stomach gave an involuntary flip and she forced herself to stay at her desk. Barney was not so self-contained, however. The puppy's ears pricked up at the sound of the front door opening, and he ran out of the office before Libby could grab him.

Worried Seth would be annoyed at being jumped up at by an overexcited puppy, she quickly followed him but found Seth crouched by Barney making a fuss of him. He seemed just as thrilled to see the dog as the dog was to see him.

"Hey," he said, looking up and seeing Libby.

"Hey," she replied, not able to prevent a smile from spreading across her face.

"Everything okay while I was away?" he asked.

"Everything's fine. How was your trip?"

"Good, I think."

He returned his attention to Barney. "Hey boy, I brought you back a present."

Barney's tail began wagging even faster. He sat when Seth asked him to, and pulled a red dinosaur soft toy out of the paper bag Seth held open for him.

"I think he likes it," said Libby laughing as the puppy ran back into her office with his prize. "I'd better go after him."

She quickly followed Barney, who'd made it through her office, and into her sitting room. She found him waiting by the back door, clearly wanting to go out in the garden, so let him out and waited until he came back in before returning to her desk to discover Seth waiting for her.

"Would you like to have supper with me tonight? I'll cook," he said.

"Are you a decent cook?" teased Libby. "I don't want to be stuck eating cold beans on burnt toast."

"I'm a very good cook," clarified Seth.

"In that case, yes, I would like to have supper with you." Butterflies began fluttering around in Libby's stomach.

"Great, I'll meet you in the kitchen at seven."

"Should I bring anything?"

"Just yourself."

Libby returned to her work, but found it very difficult to concentrate: it wasn't usual for an employer to cook their employee dinner, was it? She felt the two of them becoming closer. They certainly got along much better than they used to. Was it a good idea for them to have what could be construed as a romantic meal together though? Her feelings towards Seth were complicated enough without throwing intimate home-cooked suppers into the mix.

Well, she'd agreed to it now. It would be rude to change her mind.

Anyway, she was probably worrying about nothing. What was the likelihood that Seth Coleman would be interested in her? He was so focused on his career and curating his life, Libby was surely the antithesis of what he'd look for in a woman. But that didn't mean it wouldn't be nice to be cooked for and to spend a platonic evening with Seth. And she might as well make an effort with her appearance. She was hardly going to wear her usual relaxed evening attire of hoodie and yoga pants.

Time seemed to crawl by as Libby did her best to concentrate on Instagram posts and replying to emails while at the same time planning what she was going to wear that evening and whether she had time to wash her hair.

Finally, it was 5 p.m. She closed the lid to her computer and took Barney out for a quick run around the garden. He wasn't keen to come back in so Libby had to resort to tempting him in with some dog treats. By the time she'd given him his supper and convinced him not to eat her slippers, it was already half five.

She took her time getting ready, having a bath in her beautiful bathroom and then dressing in a blue maxi dress she loved.

At five to seven, Libby wandered through the house to the kitchen with Barney in tow, proud of herself for being on time knowing how important that was to Seth.

Delicious smells wafted from the stove top and classical piano music played gently.

"Hey," Seth said when he saw her. "You look nice."

"Thank you," Libby replied. Seth was wearing his usual uniform of black t-shirt and jeans, she noticed. Was it only for the gym that he wore anything else?

"I made you a margarita. I hope that's alright."

"That's amazing," said Libby, sinking onto one of the stools. Seth handed her a salt-rimmed drink.

"You look tired," he commented, not unkindly.

"I'm okay," she replied, taking a sip. "I've spent the afternoon sorting out tags and keywords for your website so my brain's a bit fried."

"The margarita should help, and I made some appetisers." He pushed over a plate of Manchego cheese and warm, fried chorizo.

"Thank you," Libby said, helping herself. "How was your dance practice this afternoon? Are you still getting on with Saskia?"

"It was good, thanks. Saskia's great," Seth replied, focusing intently on the griddle pan he was heating up. "Does your questioning mean that you're regretting not learning with me?"

"No, I was just wondering how it was going with you two . . ." Libby knew she wasn't being very subtle, but couldn't help it.

"Nothing is going on between me and Saskia, Libby," Seth said, making eye contact.

"Oh, I didn't mean . . ." said Libby, backpedalling.

"She's eighteen years old," Seth continued. Libby was sure he was enjoying her embarrassment at the conversational situation she'd created. "And she wouldn't be my type even if she was older. Actually, I've been meaning to tell you that I've cancelled the dance lessons. I don't have time for them."

He turned his concentration back to the food he was preparing. "I thought I'd keep it simple tonight. I've got some king prawns to grill with garlic, asparagus and walnuts."

"Sounds yummy," said Libby, fighting to hide a smile.

"It will be."

Libby smiled at his confidence, relieved that the conversation was back on neutral ground. Was there anything Seth didn't think he was brilliant at? What must it be like to be so sure of yourself all the time?

"Is there anything I can do to help?" she asked.

"You could slice up the bread."

"Sure."

Seth passed over the bread board with a knife and a loaf of ciabatta so Libby didn't have to get up.

She spotted Seth slipping a piece of cheese to Barney and couldn't help grinning.

"I think I'm nearly ready to serve up. Are you okay eating in here?"

"Of course."

Seth served everything up beautifully on a large rectangular white platter. It looked Instagram ready, and Libby wished she'd brought her camera out with her.

She spotted Seth's phone on the counter behind them. "Would you snap a photo of that?" she asked, gesturing to the food.

"I need to wash my hands. Use my phone."

"Are you sure?" Libby asked. Robert had always been very private and possessive about his mobile, and she guessed she knew why now. She liked that Seth trusted her — she knew this was his only mobile. He didn't have a more private one.

Libby took a few photos while Seth poured them each a glass of ice-cold Chablis.

"This is just as good as it looks," said Libby, tucking into the meal.

"Did you have any reason to doubt me?"

"None whatsoever," said Libby with a smile.

Once they'd finished eating and had cleared away their plates, Seth produced two individual chocolate mousses from the fridge and a bowl of strawberries.

Libby took a spoonful of the dessert. "Oh my goodness, this is so good!" she exclaimed. "Did Sarah make these?"

"No, I did," said Seth. "They only need a couple of hours to set because they're small, so I made them pretty soon after I got back earlier. I asked Sarah to get the ingredients yesterday."

So he'd planned to have dinner with her tonight. Libby wasn't sure what she thought about that, but the butterflies in her stomach definitely approved.

"I had something I wanted to talk to you about," Seth said.

"Yes?"

"It's my company's Christmas party tomorrow, and we've been let down by our photographer. Apparently she'd been double-booked. Belinda says we have to have one because someone's retiring and she's going to do photos as part of everyone's Christmas gifts . . . anyway, she hasn't been able to find anyone, and so I suggested you," he said.

"Me?" Libby replied. "But I'm not an events photographer."

"We'll pay you a thousand pounds . . ."

"I guess I'd better learn how to be an events photographer then!" said Libby, laughing, and already mentally planning what trip she could take with her new-found riches. "Thanks, Seth."

CHAPTER 10

Libby's good mood was taken down a notch the next morning when she went over the previous evening's events in her mind. The extra money from the party would be really useful, but had Seth cooked for her and been all charming and lovely just because he needed someone to photograph his party? It was a lot of trouble to go to, especially when he must have known she'd agree when he mentioned the pay. In fact, she didn't think many people would turn down money like that for a few hours of work, even if it was last minute . . . There must have been plenty of other people he could have asked.

What did it matter anyway, she decided. It was a waste of time to worry about something she was never going to know the answer to.

As soon as she'd showered and dressed, Libby opened her Mac and started binge-watching YouTube videos on event photography.

* * *

After lunch she took Barney out for a walk at a local park and then turned her focus on packing, unpacking and repacking her camera equipment. She wanted to ensure she had absolutely everything she needed, and that she could access it all quickly. It was only at 5 p.m., when she was letting Barney out for a wee, that she realised she hadn't thought about what she should wear. Although she was working at the party and wasn't a proper guest, she presumably shouldn't be wearing jeans and a t-shirt, even if Seth got away with it ninety per cent of the time.

So, an hour later, and with all the clothes she owned strewn around her bedroom, Libby had narrowed her choices down to either some smart trousers and a plain, long-sleeved top or a forest green dress with close-fitting top and a maxi tulle skirt. On reflection, the latter definitely had more of a Christmas party feel and she loved its neckline. She could move around in it fine, she told herself, and she'd feel more confident wearing it. She chose the dress.

* * *

When she got to the party venue, a large hotel ballroom, Libby was struck with nerves. What on earth made her agree to do this? The hotel was very chic, making her glad she had chosen her outfit so carefully – at least on that score she didn't look out of place, even if she felt it. Once the guests began to arrive, she soon found that everyone was so busy that, while they were polite, she was largely ignored and was able to hide behind her camera to a certain extent. The time flew by. Champagne was flowing, and she was offered several glasses, but she declined; she was too focused to drink while she was working.

She was so busy she wasn't thinking about seeing Seth, though she knew he must be there somewhere. Apparently, his secretary, Belinda, insisted he attend every year.

The guests were enjoying drinks and canapés in the bar area. Libby weaved her way around them, feeling slightly more confident now that she'd been an events photographer for more than an hour. As she snapped away at all the glamorous people in their party clothes, she couldn't help but think about how all these people worked for Seth. That was a lot of responsibility for him.

Then she felt a tap on her shoulder and turned around to find Seth standing before her. It was the first time she'd seen him out of his usual jeans and black t-shirt uniform, and she couldn't help thinking how good he looked in his suit. She took pride in it, as she'd ordered it from Armani for him a few days ago, at jaw-dropping expense. Judging by how good he looked in it, maybe designer was worth the money, though she doubted it would look so good on anyone else. She realised she was staring, probably with her mouth open judging by the peculiar look on Seth's face.

"Where's your tie?" she asked, noticing that the top button of his shirt was undone, showing a hint of dark chest hair. The pale blue tie that had arrived with the suit was missing.

Seth sheepishly pulled the tie from his jacket pocket.

Libby gave him a mock-stern look. "Aren't you going to wear it?"

"Probably not," Seth admitted. He took a sip from his champagne flute. "You look beautiful," he said.

Colour rushed to Libby's face. "Oh . . . um . . . thank you. I'd better get back to work anyway. Can't stand around here chatting all day."

She swiftly made her escape, her heart pounding.

She managed to steer clear of Seth for the next hour, though she was aware of where he was at all times. It seemed every time her eyes sought him out, he was watching her, even when he was supposedly talking to someone else.

As Libby was changing her camera lens, a small woman with dark hair and glasses approached. "I'm guessing you must be Libby," she said tentatively. "I'm Belinda, Seth's secretary."

"Oh, hi!" said Libby. "It's really good to finally meet you."

"You, too." Belinda smiled. "How are you settling in?"

"Good, I think, though there were definitely some teething problems!"

"You seem to have Seth wrapped around your little finger now. Was the puppy your idea?"

Libby laughed. "No, Barney was completely down to Seth!" she said. "I knew nothing about him until he was dropped off one morning."

"Now, that sounds like Seth. But how did you get him to agree to go to puppy training classes? I almost choked on my coffee when I saw that in Seth's schedule."

"I told him there was no point in him having a dog he wasn't going to spend any time with," Libby said.

"And you refused to learn to waltz with him?" commented Belinda. "Interesting . . ."

"In what way?"

"Most people are intimidated by Seth, at least when they first meet him."

"Oh, I was intimidated," admitted Libby.

"That's not how Seth tells it," said Belinda, giving Libby an amused look. "Looks like it's time to eat. We should be at the same table."

Libby allowed herself to be led into a large dining room next to the main hall. The room had several tables dotted around, each seating between six and ten people. The room was ornate with a huge fireplace, portraits adorning the walls and four chandeliers providing a warm light.

Libby hadn't expected to be eating with the guests, but there her name was on the seating plan, next to Seth with Belinda opposite. Her heart began beating faster again as Seth pulled out her chair for her.

"I didn't know I'd be invited to the dinner, and I definitely didn't think I'd be sitting next to you," Libby said. "Didn't you bring a date?" The woman on the other side of Seth was clearly with the man sitting on the other side of her.

"You're my date," said Seth simply. "You don't know anyone else so I asked if you could sit with me."

"Well, thank you," said Libby, touched by his thoughtfulness, though unsure how she'd get through a three-course meal next to her boss looking as good as he did in a suit.

"Can I pour you a glass of wine?" Seth asked, holding up a bottle of Sauvignon Blanc.

"I'm supposed to be working," Libby reminded him.

"I'm pretty sure you can handle one glass of wine with your food," replied Seth.

"A small one," said Libby, holding out her glass.

The meal was delicious, and Libby wandered around a fair bit photographing food and people, though making sure she tried to never catch anyone chewing. She couldn't help noticing that Seth's attention was completely on her whenever she returned to the table. He introduced her to everyone at the seated around them and to anyone who came over to talk to him, telling them all what a talented photographer she was.

Once the meal was over, people began moving back through to the ballroom where the music was starting up, and Libby followed them in, camera in hand.

Libby was due to clock off at midnight, but at eleven, she felt another tap on her shoulder and turned to find Seth with two glasses of champagne. He held one out to her.

"I can't, I'm working!" she said, firmly, though she couldn't help smiling.

"Do you honestly think anyone wants their photo taken right now? They're all drunk. It's time for you to clock off."

Libby had to agree that most people were definitely looking a little worse for wear.

She accepted the drink.

"Are you having a good night?"

"Some of it's been good," Seth replied. His gaze seemed to linger on her. *Was he flirting?*

"How come you're the only person here who's not drunk?"

"You're not drunk either."

"I'm working."

"I'll let you in on a little secret," Seth said, leaning in. His smell filled her nostrils and the image of them waltzing together flooded her brain. "I'm very good at appearing sober when I'm actually not."

Libby decided not to mention that he was definitely standing closer to her than he normally would. Not that she was doing anything to move away.

"Shall I give you a hand packing up your equipment?" Seth asked.

Libby's heart sank. She wasn't ready for this moment to end and for it to be time for her to leave.

"Sure, thanks," she managed to murmur.

"And then," Seth said, "I'd like you to dance with me."

Libby's jaw dropped. "Didn't you learn your lesson from our attempt at waltzing?" she replied.

"I guess I'm just a sucker for punishment." He grinned. Then, seeing the uncertainty on Libby's face, he said, "Please. I've managed to avoid the dance floor all night, but Belinda tells me I need to get out there. Don't make me go alone."

Libby sighed. "Fine, okay."

* * *

The next morning, Libby wandered into the kitchen with Barney to get some late breakfast and was surprised to see Seth sitting at the breakfast bar with a cup of coffee in his hands.

"Oh! Hi," Libby said. "Sorry, I didn't mean to disturb your breakfast."

"You're not. I had my breakfast a while ago. I was just having a coffee, and you live here, so this is your kitchen too."

"Okay."

"Did you enjoy yourself last night?"

"I did," Libby said. "Thanks for hiring me for it, and for taking me under your wing."

"It was my pleasure," said Seth. "I have to admit, I may have drunk a little more than I thought. My head's a bit sore this morning. Um . . . I hope you didn't feel pressured into dancing with me by the way. I thought it would be fun, but I was being selfish not wanting to go out onto the dance floor by myself . . ."

"I didn't feel pressured," Libby reassured him. "You're a good dance partner."

"Your dancing isn't nearly as bad as I remember, I knew you were putting it on when we did that waltz class."

Libby laughed. "You'll never know," she teased.

Seth got up. "I'll be heading out in a bit. I can take Barney and give him a walk on my way back."

"He'll like that," said Libby.

"Come on then, Barney," said Seth. "Let's get your lead."

"Do you need his crate? Because the Mercedes is still at the hotel." Libby blushed as she remembered Seth ordering an Uber for them both when the party ended and holding the door of it open for her when it arrived.

"Jamie picked up your car for you this morning, it's in the garage."

"On a Sunday?"

"Don't worry, he didn't mind," said Seth. "And I paid him well. But I don't need the crate. I got Barney a harness and a seatbelt I thought I'd try out. That way he can sit in the front with me."

"Oh, okay. Have fun!" said Libby, grinning at how cute Barney looked following his master out of the room.

The weather was disgusting so Libby was happy to spend the day relaxing in her flat without even having to walk Barney, especially as she hadn't got home until after 2 a.m.

But she couldn't help wondering what yesterday had meant. Had Seth been flirting with her? Or had she been imagining it? Maybe he was just naturally like that with women. Or the alcohol he'd drunk. She definitely shouldn't read too much into it, she decided. But it was hard when all she could think about was the feeling of his body against hers when they were dancing.

CHAPTER 11

On Monday, Libby spent the morning sorting through and editing the photographs from the Christmas party and sent them off to Seth and Belinda before lunch. Events would never be her favourite thing to photograph, but she was pleased with what she'd captured.

About half an hour before they were due to leave for puppy class, Libby got a text message from Seth: *Not sure I'll be able to make Barney's class this evening. Bit snowed under.*

Libby snorted to herself and immediately typed back: *You're coming, Coleman. Just watch your ankles better this week.*

As soon as she'd sent it she worried she'd gone too far, and was relieved when another message arrived almost immediately.

Okay. But I'm wearing waterproofs.

Barney was much more confident going into the hall and began playing with his new friends straight away. Seth, however, was wary and was clearly keeping his distance from the puppies as much as possible. Libby noticed him beginning to relax after a while though, and how proud he looked of Barney when he won a treat for how well he sat and waited.

"We're having an extra fundraising event on Saturday," Judith explained at the end of the class. "It's a fun dog show

114

followed by mince pies and mulled wine. We'd love for all the puppies to enter, and there will be some special categories just for them. There's a list of the categories for you to grab by the door on your way out."

Libby picked up the information sheet as they were leaving and smiled as she read the categories. Of course, she decided, Barney would have to enter.

Seth pretended to be nonchalant until they were in the car. "Show me the list!" he said eagerly. Libby handed over the piece of paper.

"You're so competitive," she moaned.

"And what's wrong with that?" replied Seth. "It'll be good for his self-esteem when he wins."

"I think his self-esteem is just fine."

Seth ignored as he studied the categories. "What on earth is a waggiest tail competition? How do they even judge that?" He looked at Barney's tail which started wagging even faster under his master's appraisal.

"Don't get any ideas," said Libby, shaking her head. "Barney doesn't stand a chance in that category. There's a Pomeranian who wags her tail so hard that sometimes she falls over. It's adorable."

"So, what shall we enter Barney into? We should get practising for the categories he stands the best chance in. We've only got a few days."

"Seth," Libby said in a mock-exasperated voice. "It's just a bit of fun to raise money to fix the centre's roof."

"Sure, but we want him to perform to the best of his potential."

Libby sighed.

"Cutest puppy is a shoo-in, of course," Seth mumbled to himself.

"But what about that Alsatian, Toby?" Libby teased. "He's pretty cute."

Barney and Seth turned as one to face her. Libby bit her bottom lip to stop herself from laughing at the pair of them with almost identical disgruntled expressions on their faces.

"You think Toby is cuter than Barney?" asked Seth, incredulously. He put his hand protectively on the dog's head.

"No, of course not!" replied Libby, firmly retrieving the dog show information from Seth. "Anyway, we should get going. You've got a conference call in half an hour, and you need to get ready."

Seth opened his mouth to argue, but Libby said firmly, "I'll enter him in plenty of categories, but we have to let the other dogs have a chance to win something too."

"Fine," agreed Seth, somewhat reluctantly it seemed. "But make sure you get him an appointment at the groomers for the morning of the competition."

"Okay," said Libby, letting Seth believe he'd won a point. As if she wasn't going to get Barney groomed before his big competition. He was going to blow those other dogs out of the water.

* * *

Once they were back, Seth went straight back to work. Libby made herself a baked potato in the microwave and did her best to ignore the disappointment she felt that he wasn't joining her for dinner. She took her food into her flat, settled down in front of Netflix and was pleased Barney was so tired that he fell asleep in his basket almost straight away.

* * *

Seth had scheduled a short meeting with her the following day and Libby reprimanded herself when she caught herself checking her appearance in the mirror before she went up to see him. *You're such a cliché*, she scolded. *Getting a crush on an older, wealthy man, just after you've broken up with your boyfriend! Get over it, you've got far too much to lose if you mess this job up!*

"Hi, Libby! Where's Barney?" Seth said when she went into his office.

"He's downstairs, I didn't think it was worth bringing him up."

Seth nodded, though he looked disappointed.

"I'll bring him next time," Libby promised. "What can I do for you?"

"You did a fantastic job on Saturday night. Everyone's thrilled with the results."

"Oh, great."

"So, I have a business acquaintance who needs a photographer . . ."

"Right . . ." said Libby, warily. Where was he going with this?

"And I'm emailing you the details of the job," Seth continued.

"Aren't you happy with my work?" asked Libby, momentarily panicked. Was Seth trying to get rid of her?

"Of course, I am," said Seth immediately. "This is just a small job. You could do it over a weekend or take some holiday. I just thought it would get you more photography experience."

"But . . . I wasn't after more photography experience," Libby said, taken aback. "Are the photos I've taken for your social media not good enough?" She knew she was getting defensive, but she couldn't seem to help herself.

Seth looked momentarily flustered. "Your photos are perfect. This job would help to build up your portfolio though."

"But I don't need a portfolio, because I don't want to be a photographer," Libby said. "I studied photography in college. I love it, but I wouldn't want to do it for a job full-time."

"Alright, but it's a brilliant opportunity!"

"Seth," said Libby firmly, "I'm not one of your projects!"

"I know you're not. I'm trying to help."

"Thank you, but I don't need your help, I can run my own life. Just because I don't set ninety-day productivity goals and down raw eggs several times a day doesn't mean I'm failing."

Seth frowned. "I never said you were failing . . . I just meant that . . ."

"You implied it."

They glared at each other.

"I don't want to be a photographer."

"Are you even going to look at the details of the job?"

"No. Can I get back to my *actual* job now, please? I need to walk your dog."

"Of course," said Seth, turning away with a shrug.

Libby turned and walked out of Seth's office and down the stairs to her own workspace with as much authority as she could muster.

She grabbed Barney's lead and called the puppy to her. He leapt excitedly off the sofa — he definitely knew the signal for walkies.

Clipping the lead onto Barney's collar, Libby headed out of her sitting room's French doors, around the house, and out of the garden. She contemplated taking the car, but she just wanted to walk. She needed to clear her head.

She marched along the tree-lined avenues, past the gates behind which sat mansions of various sizes and tastes until she realised she was giving poor Barney no chance to sniff and explore. She slowed down: it wasn't Barney's fault his master was a controlling idiot.

Seth was so frustrating — why was he always trying to improve her? To change her and push her into whatever direction he deemed most suitable for her? Why couldn't he just leave her to make her own stupid decisions? What difference did it make to him if she messed up her life anyway?

It was bad enough feeling that her parents thought she was a failure, without Seth doing the same.

What did she care what Seth thought about her? She worked for him, that's all. It was probably really inappropriate for him to be interfering in her life.

And he was just so interfering! Just because he chose to live his life like a crazy person, setting goals and challenges for himself every thirty seconds, didn't give him the right to inflict the same insanity upon her. She stomped on.

After half an hour, Libby had calmed down enough to return to her desk. She logged into her email, and unexpectedly, as it wasn't 9 a.m., found she had a message from Seth with no subject. As much as she didn't want to open it, he was her boss, so she clicked. It was the details of the photography job, for a new hotel opening outside Paris in a few months. She'd be flown out and would stay in the hotel for the weekend so she could take photos for their website and promo material. It was an amazing opportunity, and the pay was brilliant. Libby put her head in her hands.

* * *

Fed up with her own company, Libby decided to take a break and headed into the kitchen where Sarah was making Thai green curry.

"Hey, what's up?" Sarah asked as soon as she saw Libby's face.

"I'm alright," said Libby.

"Seth's also wandering around like a bear with a sore head, so I'm guessing that's got something to do with it."

Libby sighed. "Seth tried to set me up with another photography job and I didn't react well," she admitted.

"Why not?" asked Sarah gently.

Libby laughed bitterly. "Well, to begin with, I thought he was trying to get rid of me," she confessed, "but then I felt he was trying to push me into doing something he thinks is good for me. I've had people do that before and it's something I'm touchy about, I guess."

"I'm sure he was only trying to help you."

"I know."

"Seth can't help trying to bring out the best in people. It's what his charity does and his charity is an extension of him. He won't have told you that he pays for my son, Ethan, to go to private school. When he found out that Ethan was struggling

119

at school, Seth had his assessment for dyslexia fast-tracked and, when it was revealed that was the problem, he offered to pay the fees for Ethan to go to the school with the best facilities to help him. A school I'd never be able to afford."

"That was kind of him," said Libby.

"It was," agreed Sarah, "But it took a lot of persuading to get me to accept his offer. I only did so because it was for Ethan. I'm very glad I did though. He's thrived in his new school."

"That's great."

"And Jamie was expelled from school when he was sixteen. Thankfully, one of his teachers got in touch with Seth's charity. Seth put him through horticultural college and then offered him the job here."

"I had no idea."

"Don't worry, Jamie won't mind me telling you, but Seth doesn't advertise this stuff. What I'm trying to say," continued Sarah, "is don't take it personally. Seth has a lot of money, and he likes to use it to help people. He will have thought he was doing the right thing."

"Okay, thanks," said Libby. "I think I need to speak to Seth."

Before she could think better of it, Libby headed back up to Seth's office and knocked on the door. There was silence, and she was about to turn around and leave when she heard Seth say, "Yes?"

Libby pushed open the door.

"Is everything alright?" Seth asked, looking up from his computer screen.

"Yes," said Libby. "I'm sorry. And I know I'm supposed to make an appointment to see you, but I feel really bad about what I said, and I needed to apologise now. You were only trying to help me, and I was rude."

"Thank you," said Seth. "In fairness, I was maybe being a tiny bit pushy, but you've said you don't want to be a photographer, so I'll leave you alone."

"I get defensive because I know my parents wish I would settle down with a steady job and they're always suggesting things they think I should do, and my ex, the one whose house I was moving out of, used to email me with jobs he thought I should apply for, even when I'd already said I wasn't interested. And I get frustrated with myself. Is it normal to not know what you want to do other than travel? And to flit between different jobs all the time?"

"Everyone's different, and you've got to make your own choices," Seth said. "And, for the record, I don't want you to get another job."

"I don't want to either," said Libby. "Sarah was telling me about everything you've done for her son and Jamie."

"I gave them a helping hand, that's all. They did all the hard work themselves. But I wanted to talk to you about that. I was wondering if you'd like to get involved more in the charity as part of your job, in particular helping to decide who we support."

"I'd really like that," said Libby.

"Good, I'll get Belinda to send you some details."

"Thanks," said Libby. She turned to leave.

"Libby?" Seth said.

"Yes?"

"You don't need to make an appointment to see me anymore."

"Oh," said Libby, surprised. "Are you sure?"

"Yes, if it's important. But don't let anyone else know. They'll all be turning up and I won't get a moment's peace."

"I won't tell," said Libby.

She went down the stairs, grinning to herself and almost bumped into Sarah.

"I take it you've made up with Seth," Sarah said with a laugh.

"Yep!" said Libby, happily. "And I've been awarded special privileges," she called out over her shoulder.

"I can't say I'm surprised," Sarah muttered under her breath as she watched Libby go into her office.

* * *

Libby called Belinda straight away.

"How much do you know about the charity already?" Belinda asked.

"Just that it's aimed at teenagers, and that the help is tailored to their needs."

"Yes, teenagers and their families as well if they also need some support. Basically, it's kept as simple as possible. There's no formal application procedure. Seth asks everyone to let him know if there are any teens they hear of who need help. Then you'll chat with Seth about the best way to help that teen. Sometimes it's money, sometimes a job, finding the right course for them and giving them a hand filling in application forms . . . it depends on the individual case. Seth doesn't like to make a fuss about it, and he doesn't want the kids to have to jump through hoops to get help. There's no publicity allowed."

"Why's that? It seems it would be good for the charity to receive publicity?"

"Seth didn't grow up with much," explained Belinda. "He says he would have hated to have been photographed receiving a handout, so he doesn't want to put anyone else through that."

"Oh," said Libby. She'd known Seth had built his business up from nothing but hadn't realised his family had struggled.

"I'll send you some more information in the next few days," said Belinda, "And look out for an email from me in a minute."

"Alright, thanks Belinda," said Libby.

Libby returned to her computer planning to reply to the email about the photography job, but she was distracted by the email coming through from Belinda. *Check you out!* said the subject line. Libby opened the email revealing a photo of her and Seth dancing. She hadn't realised it had been taken. She was resting her head on Seth's shoulder with her arms around Seth's neck. His hand rested on her waist, and he was saying something into her ear. They looked like they weren't aware of anyone else in the room.

Libby smiled for a second and then sighed, and her good mood evaporated. What was she getting herself into? She was falling for someone she knew she could never be with! Why would a successful, driven businessman want to be with someone like her? A temp who couldn't look further than her next holiday destination! Not to mention the fact that she worked for him! She had to snap out of this infatuation before it ended up causing her real problems.

Her phone dinged with a message. From Robert. Libby debated deleting it without opening it, but something stopped her.

Hi Libby, I miss you. I miss us. And I hate what I did to us. Would you have dinner with me tomorrow night? I just want to talk. Robert x

Libby stared at the message for a long time. She had to admit that she didn't feel a full sense of closure over their relationship. They'd been together for so long, shared so many experiences together, and all that was just wiped out by his stupid mistake. They hadn't even talked properly. She'd said goodbye to their home, but not to him. She found herself replying: *Okay*.

CHAPTER 12

The next few days were filled with trying to stop Seth from spending every spare minute he had preparing Barney for the dog show. The poor puppy would be exhausted by the time it came around.

The dog show was due to start at 3 p.m., so Libby took Barney to the dog groomers at 12, having taken him for a walk beforehand. No way was that puppy getting mucky before his competition.

Libby was getting everything ready to go when she stopped and smiled to herself. She never in a million years would have thought that she'd love a job so much that involved her going to a dog show at a local community hall on a Saturday as part of her duties. It was certainly true that you were never bored when you worked for Seth! And Barney had turned out to be a wonderful perk of the job. She'd miss Barney when she went to her parents for Christmas. She'd miss Seth too. It didn't seem like he'd be having much of a Christmas at all, which seemed a shame. She'd asked if he wanted her to decorate the house for him and organise a tree, but he'd told her not to bother.

"Are you ready to go?" Seth called out impatiently from the hallway.

"It's not even half past yet!" Libby shouted back.

"We don't want to be late!" came the reply.

Muttering darkly to herself, under her breath, Libby shoved some dog treats into her bag and hurried through to Seth. Barney ran ahead of her, thrilled to hear his master's voice.

"You look good!" said Seth, picking the puppy up. "Who's the cutest doggo in the whole world?"

Libby screwed up her face. "Don't do that," she said, firmly.

"Well, he is," said Seth, though he did have the good grace to look embarrassed. "Come on, let's go!"

"Alright!" said Libby. "But carry him out to the car. I don't want to risk him finding some mud to roll in."

* * *

When they arrived at the show, Libby waved at the people she knew from puppy classes. Seth looked stiff and uncomfortable, his eyes scanning the hall and its occupants.

"You're checking out the competition, aren't you?" Libby whispered.

"Of course, I am," muttered Seth. "Are those bows in that Yorkie's hair?"

"Looks like it."

"Should we have done that for Barney?"

"No!" hissed Libby, firmly.

"Where do we enter him?" Seth asked, suitably rebuked.

"It's already done," said Libby, managing to hide the grin managing to spread across her face. "They asked people to email with the categories they wanted their dog to enter so they knew how many dogs would be in each category."

"Which categories did you choose?" demanded Seth, his brow furrowed.

"Oh, look, there's Judith," said Libby, pointedly ignoring him. "I must go over to say hello and see if she needs help with anything."

She knew she was being cruel, but she'd only let him suffer for a few minutes before she showed him she'd entered Barney in as many categories as she could, including one very special one she was sure he'd win.

The hall had been decorated for the party. An enormous Christmas tree stood in a corner, which all the dog owners endeavoured to keep their charges away from. Judith explained that the paper chains hung around the walls had been made by a Beaver Scout group, and the sewing group had made bunting which was placed above the doors and windows. The local WI group were manning the refreshments, and Libby left Barney with Seth while she went to get them some mulled wine and mince pies.

She returned to find Seth still checking out the competition and handed him his plastic cup of mulled wine. "I'm not sure alcohol's the best idea," Seth muttered.

Libby laughed. "It's half a cup and it's not you competing. All you've got to do is stand there with him."

"What! I thought you'd be taking him in the competitions," said Seth, his face turning pale.

"I have no idea where you got that idea from," said Libby. "He's your dog and you're down as his owner for the classes."

Seth downed his mulled wine in one. "Okay, then Barney," he said. "Let's show them who the best dog here is."

Libby found herself a seat where she had a perfect view to experience Seth's discomfort in all its glory.

Barney did well at titbit catching, which came as no surprise, and picked up a third-place ribbon. It was Seth's fault Barney didn't place in the waggiest tail category — he didn't get Barney excited enough. Next came Best Rescue and Best Veteran dog, which Libby obviously hadn't entered Barney into, so Seth came over to join her. Libby congratulated Barney.

"He should have got first for the titbits," muttered Seth. "He got distracted."

"There was some tough competition," pointed out Libby. "I can't believe you didn't get his tail wagging more!

You should have told him how handsome he is; he loves that!"

"I wasn't going to do that in front of everyone!"

"You lost him a rosette!"

"Don't worry," replied Seth, his jaw set. "There are plenty more for us to win."

Seth and Barney went back for Most Beautiful Eyes, which Barney won second prize for, much to Libby's delight, and Seth's rather obvious disappointment. Next was the category Libby had been waiting for: Grumpiest Owner. Seth's scowl over at Libby when he realised what he'd been entered in gained him first prize.

Barney got too distracted in the hoop jumping category, but then, finally it was time for Best in Show. The judges walked around the inside of the circle of dogs and their owners, asking the occasional question before they went off to confer. Finally, they came back to make their announcement. Judith did the honours and declared, "Third place goes to Charlie, second place to Rover and the first place in the Best in Show category goes to . . . Barney!"

Libby whooped with delight, and catching Seth's eyes, she knew she was forgiven for her little trick.

* * *

Before they left the party, the dogs were each given a present. Seth helped Barney to open his and got a very excited lick right on his nose when Barney discovered he'd been given a new ball with an extremely loud squeaker. "That one's going to have to disappear," Seth muttered, as if Barney could understand.

"Good luck getting it off him," said Libby.

Judith came over as they were leaving. "Thank you both so much for coming. We're hoping the money raised this evening will at least make the council reconsider selling the hall."

They walked out to the car together, Barney proudly carrying his treasured new ball.

"Wasn't Barney brilliant?" said Seth. "We'll have to find a place to display all his rosettes. Could you order some kind of display case?"

"Sure," Libby said. She had to admit, Barney did look very pleased with himself, but she suspected that was more down to the huge number of treats he'd consumed in the past couple of hours than anything else.

"Let's go out to celebrate!" said Seth. "There's a nice dog-friendly pub in Walton-on-Thames. Why don't I make us a reservation for 8 o'clock?"

"That sounds lovely, but I'm going out tonight," said Libby.

"You've got a date?" asked Seth, looking a bit deflated.

"Kind of," said Libby.

Seth looked at her questioningly. She gave a little sigh and continued, "I'm meeting my ex, Robert. The one whose house you helped me move out of. He says he wants to talk."

"You're getting back together with him," said Seth, slowly.

"No, I didn't say that," explained Libby.

"Then why are you going out for supper with him?"

"It's complicated . . ."

"He cheated on you," said Seth, bluntly.

Libby tried to control her temper. "I know, but everyone makes mistakes."

"Well, you're making a mistake going out with him."

"It's my mistake to make and it's not really any of your business," Libby retorted.

"Friends are honest with each other and that's all I'm trying to be."

"We're friends now, are we?" she scoffed.

Seth hesitated. "I hoped so."

"Friends support their friends even when they don't agree with their friends' decisions."

"I can't do that," said Seth.

"I guess we're not friends then," said Libby, and they drove home in silence.

* * *

Libby stomped about getting ready. She didn't feel like going and hashing everything out with Robert, but if she cancelled and stayed at home, Seth would think he'd won.

She stopped herself and took a few deep breaths. She was doing this so that she could at least get some closure from her relationship with Robert. And if he wanted to get back together, she could at least hear him out.

Libby changed into a blue jersey dress she knew Robert liked and did her make-up extra carefully. She may as well feel her best when she went to face her cheating ex.

Seth was in the kitchen with Barney when she emerged from her flat. Barney came over and she gave him a stroke.

"I'm off," she called out.

Seth stood at the counter, pouring himself a glass of wine. "Okay. Barney, come!" He looked up and caught her eye.

All of a sudden, Libby had an almost irresistible urge to stay with Seth. To sit with him in his beautiful kitchen and talk about Barney while he cooked.

She shook her head. She needed to go to meet Robert.

* * *

Robert had booked a table at an Italian restaurant they both used to like. He spotted her as soon as she walked in and waved.

Libby made her way through the tightly packed restaurant, made even cosier by the large Christmas tree in the corner covered in hundreds of multicoloured lights and baubles. "I'm so glad you came," Robert said, standing when she approached. "I wasn't sure you would."

"Neither was I," Libby admitted, taking a seat.

He sat down again. He looked his usual self: smart and classically tall, dark and handsome. Libby was taken back to when she'd first been introduced to him at a party thrown by a mutual friend. She almost hadn't believed it when he'd asked for her number after they'd chatted in a corner about their shared love of travel for most of the party.

"You look beautiful," he said, running his eyes over her and bringing Libby's thoughts back to the present.

"Thank you," she said, embarrassed under his scrutiny.

A waiter came over and took their drink orders. "Shall we share a bottle of red?" Robert suggested.

"I'll just have a sparkling water, thanks," Libby replied. She wanted to keep her wits about her. She was feeling particularly vulnerable after her argument with Seth, and alcohol wasn't a good idea. She wanted to keep her defences well and truly up. Plus, she needed to be able to drive herself home later.

"So, how have you been?" Robert asked.

"Good," said Libby. "I've got a new job."

Robert laughed. "What are you doing this week?"

Libby ignored him. She was used to blocking out those kinds of comments. "I'm a sort of girl Friday to Seth Coleman, the property developer."

"Seth Coleman, eh? What's he like?"

"A little unusual," admitted Libby. "But I like it there. It's interesting."

"Where are you living now?"

"With Seth," Libby answered. "I mean, the job is live-in. I have my own flat in his house."

"So you see a lot of him, then?"

"Yes."

Robert seemed to think better about questioning Libby about her relationship with Seth. "Shall we order?" he said.

* * *

A couple of hours later and they had both relaxed more in each other's company.

"Thank you so much for agreeing to this," Robert said as the waiter cleared away their pudding plates. "It's good to see you."

"And you," admitted Libby. Robert was charming and funny; he was easy to spend time with. It was all too simple to allow herself to forget, at least momentarily, how their relationship had ended.

"Libby," Robert said, reaching across to hold her hand. "I am so incredibly sorry for what I did. I don't know what I was thinking. I was a complete idiot."

"Yes, you were."

"She meant nothing to me, and it only happened the once," he continued. "Honestly, I think I got scared. We got together young and the next step for us was to get married. I wanted to marry you, but I freaked out."

"At the thought of marrying me?"

"At the thought of getting married full stop. It was nothing to do with you. I love you."

"I loved you too, Robert . . ."

"I don't expect you to forgive me straight away," Robert said. "God knows, I'll never forgive myself. But would you consider giving us another chance? We were really good together, Lib." Robert stared at her beseechingly.

Libby's heart pounded in her chest. She'd expected something like this, but being faced with it threw all her previous debating about what she would do out of the window.

Yes, Robert had messed up royally, but no one was perfect. They'd been good together, and the thought of returning to the little house and the life they'd shared together was kind of . . . comforting. And he said he'd only cheated on her once. Did that make a difference? Did she believe that? She couldn't be sure.

"There's no need to answer me tonight," Robert said. "Take your time, and we can talk more soon. Perhaps we could do this again?"

Libby nodded, too much going through her mind for her to form words.

They walked together out of the restaurant and to where the Mercedes was parked. Robert whistled, "Nice ride," he said. "How on earth did you afford this?"

"It's not mine," explained Libby. "It comes with the job."

Robert looked momentarily put out but recovered quickly.

"I'll call you," he said and, almost before she realised what was happening, kissed Libby lightly on the lips. Then he turned and walked away and Libby, mind whirling, got into the car.

CHAPTER 13

Libby arranged to meet Melissa for brunch on Sunday morning. She'd been looking forward to it since her argument with Seth and unsettling supper with Robert.

She knew a lot of what Seth said was true, but it annoyed her that she'd carried his opinions with her into her meal with Robert. That didn't seem fair. Not that Robert necessarily deserved to be treated fairly.

She was giving Barney a little run in the garden before she put him safely in his crate and promised him she wouldn't be long. She didn't like leaving him, but dogs weren't allowed in the restaurant. She heard Seth call her name and turned round to find him coming out of the house to speak to her.

"I'm off out a bit later," said Seth, stiffly. "I thought I'd take Barney with me if that's alright with you."

"That's fine. He is your dog," Libby pointed out.

"I know, but you do so much for him, I feel I should check."

"Well, it's very nice of you to do so. I was going to leave him here, but it would be easier if you had him. I'm going soon though."

"That's fine. He can hang with me until I'm ready to go," Seth said.

"Great." She shrugged. "I guess I'll see you both later then. Have a good day."

Seth looked at her and went to turn before spinning back to face her. "Libby, I hate when there's an atmosphere between us," he blurted out. "And it's none of my business who you choose to be romantically involved with."

"You're right there," replied Libby.

"It's just . . ." began Seth before shaking his head.

"What?" said Libby.

"Nothing," said Seth. "Can we be friends again and I'll do my best to stay out of your love life?"

Libby's chest clenched at the realisation that that was the last thing she wanted him to do, but she nodded. "Sure, that would be good."

Seth left, leaving Libby feeling unsettled and once again frustrated that she didn't know where he went on his Sunday excursions. Why did it matter so much that she didn't know, she wondered as she drove into Weybridge. She guessed it was because the rest of his life was such an open book, or an open spreadsheet rather. She generally knew what Seth was going to be doing at any given time of any given day. Why was he so secretive? Maybe he had a second home and spent his day slobbing around in front of the television watching rubbish and eating junk food. She giggled at the thought — it seemed pretty unlikely.

* * *

Thoughts of Seth and his mysterious whereabouts were pushed to the back of her mind by the delicious scrambled eggs and avocado on toast and freshly squeezed orange juice she had for brunch.

In the end, she couldn't face the thought of getting into an argument with someone else about her meeting up for dinner with Robert and decided not to say anything about it to Melissa. She was still more than a little unsure about what she was doing herself. She'd take some time to work out her own feelings and then share them with her friend. Instead, she found herself telling Melissa about Barney and the dog show and how much training Seth had been doing with him for it.

"So he's not quite the robot he comes across as then," said Melissa.

"He's not a robot at all," said Libby, swiftly rising to Seth's defence. "He's driven and focused, but that doesn't mean he can't also be kind and thoughtful."

Melissa's eyebrows raised. "Okay, fair enough," she said. "I'm glad you're getting on well with him."

"Barney has definitely helped with that," said Libby with a smile.

She looked over at her friend who was giving her a questioning look. "There's nothing going on between you two, is there?" Melissa said.

"No, of course not!" said Libby immediately. "We're friends, that's all. There's no way he'd be interested in someone like me, even if I did like him like that, which I don't! I mean, can you imagine dating someone that regimented? It would drive you crazy . . ."

But something about the expression on Melissa's face told her she wasn't completely convinced by what Libby was saying, and she didn't think her friend was either.

An hour later, Libby hugged Melissa goodbye and walked back to the car. She was pulling out of the car park when she saw Seth driving past. Without pausing to consider her actions, Libby turned in the opposite direction to St George's Hill and began to follow him.

She kept a little way back, but luckily, though the roads were busy, his car was easy to keep sight of. He only drove for a few minutes before turning down into a quiet cul-de-sac and parking up.

Libby stopped her own car on the main road so that he was in view and watched him get out of his car, put a lead on Barney, and walk with the puppy up to the front door of a little semi-detached cottage. The door opened, but she couldn't see who was inside, and Seth and Barney went inside the house.

What could Seth be doing here? It was a very nice, if perfectly ordinary street, not the kind of place she imagined Seth would visit. And what was she going to do now? It wasn't like she was planning to sit in her car until whatever time Seth decided to leave. He was usually out for several hours . . . Not that she'd planned to spend her Sunday like this anyway! What exactly was she doing? She was acting like a complete lunatic. She had no right to follow her boss. What business was it of hers anyway what Seth did on Sundays? She had no idea what any of her previous employers had done on the weekend and honestly had no interest in finding out.

But deep down, Libby knew Seth was different. She hadn't been able to stop herself from following him here. It was like she needed to know everything about him. But she must leave now. Her behaviour was creepy and it needed to stop immediately.

She took out her phone and opened Google maps. She'd been so busy concentrating on following Seth, she now had no idea where she was. Maybe she shouldn't go straight home; she'd only spend the afternoon going over why she'd followed him and feeling guilty about it . . . but what could she do instead?

The tap on the car window made Libby jump. She turned and found Seth standing next to her car, staring through the glass at her. Barney was at his feet, excitedly trying to jump up at the car door.

She wound down the window and sheepishly said, "Hi."

"So, I brought Barney outside for a minute, and imagine my surprise when I spotted your car . . . What exactly are you doing here?" asked Seth tersely.

Libby considered lying, but what would be the point? She couldn't think of anything that would sound even remotely plausible.

"I followed you," she admitted.

"Why would you do that?"

"I don't know. I didn't plan to," Libby explained. "You drove past, and I followed you. I guess I was curious . . ."

"Why didn't you ask me what I was doing if you were so curious?"

"I didn't think you'd tell me. You seem really secretive about what you do on Sundays."

He frowned. "Aren't I allowed to keep my private life private?"

"Yes, of course you are, and again, I am so sorry. I don't know what came over me."

Seth was silent for a moment. "Come on," he eventually said. He opened the car door for Libby to climb out. "I've got to get back. I only came out to grab something from my car."

Libby followed Seth to his car where he picked up a large bunch of flowers from the front passenger seat. He led her to the house he'd gone into before. Libby stalled, embarrassed.

"Come on," repeated Seth. "It's okay. It's really not a huge secret."

They went into the house. It was tastefully decorated and more modern inside than Libby had expected. Barney came running out to the hallway to greet them and was thrilled to see Libby.

"Through here," said Seth, and they walked past a door leading to a sitting room. The kitchen-diner was at the back of the house. A woman was putting a roasting pan in the oven.

"Mum, we have a guest," Seth said, and she turned around. Seth's mother was small and smiley, with grey hair tied back in a loose bun, and she wore an apron covering her stripy top and jeans.

"Libby, this is my mother, Ann. Mum, this is Libby, my personal assistant. She just happened to be passing and I thought you'd like to meet her."

Libby smiled, grateful Seth had covered up for her when he so easily could have made things even more awkward.

"It's lovely to meet you, Libby," said Ann, wiping her hands. "You'll stay for lunch, won't you? I always cook far too much!"

"Oh no, thank you, but . . ." began Libby.

"I'm sure Libby has plenty to do," Seth continued for her. He looked as surprised as she was at his mother's invitation.

"Well, can I at least make you a nice cup of tea then?" Ann asked.

Libby looked at Seth to see what she should do but his face was expressionless and she didn't want to be rude to his mother. "A cup of tea would be lovely," she said.

* * *

Libby left half an hour later very surprised at what a nice time she'd had. Seth's mother was charming; so friendly, warm and open. She'd almost wished she hadn't turned down the invitation of food, as it smelled delicious and Ann was so easy to talk to, but she didn't think Seth would be at all happy with her staying longer. She didn't want to annoy him even more than she had already that day.

Rather than heading home, she drove to Weybridge station and took a train into London to see an exhibition at the V&A — thrilled with herself for doing something so cultural in her free time. She couldn't remember the last time she'd been to a museum or gallery. Going to those sorts of places wasn't something Robert had enjoyed doing and so she'd got out of the habit.

On her return to the house, she waited anxiously for Seth to get home, wondering if he'd been stewing over what she'd done and if he was crosser than he'd been earlier.

Finally, she heard his car stopping outside the house and a moment later there was a knock on the door to her flat.

Barney jumped up to greet her as soon as she opened the door.

"Is it alright if I leave him with you for the evening?" Seth asked, without saying hello. "I was going to do a session in the gym."

"Yes, that's fine," said Libby.

Seth turned to go, but Libby couldn't leave things unsaid. She'd feel even worse about her actions if she allowed her guilt to fester. Plus, she needed to know the extent of Seth's anger over her following him.

"About earlier," she began awkwardly.

"Are you referring to you stalking me?"

"I wasn't stalking you!" Libby snapped. She couldn't tell if he was angry or teasing her.

"What would you call it then?"

"I followed you *one* time. I shouldn't have, and I've apologised for it, but I wanted to check you're not too mad at me."

Seth gave a little laugh. "I'm not mad at you," he said. "Although I should be. You have got to be the nosiest person I have ever met."

"It's not one of my finest qualities," Libby admitted.

"My visiting my mother every week isn't some sort of huge secret. I just choose not to share it with my employees because, frankly, it's none of your business and because I'm very protective over her."

"That's completely fair enough, and it will never happen again."

"As it happens, my mother loved you and would like you to visit again soon," Seth said with a smile. "I can't say I see what she thought was so great, but there you are."

Libby's face broke into a grin, "She liked me?" she said.

"She did," Seth confirmed. "Is that important to you?"

"It's nice to be liked," said Libby, defensively, but it was good to know she was approved of by Seth's mother, although she couldn't for the life of her explain why that would make a difference to anything . . .

CHAPTER 14

Libby and Barney went to puppy class by themselves on Monday evening as Seth had been locked in his office with back-to-back meetings. He hadn't even been able to make Barney Time and Libby hadn't seen him all day. He still had a late meeting and Libby accepted it would be awkward for him to get out of it.

Barney was very excited when Libby pulled into the community centre's car park. He was wriggling around so much, it was hard to unclip him from his harness and get his lead on.

However, when they got inside, it was clear there was something wrong. Everyone was huddled together in the centre of the hall, talking urgently, their puppies still on their leads.

"What's going on?" Libby asked, joining the group.

"The hall's been sold," said Judith, sadly. "It's going to be knocked down and turned into yet more office buildings."

"Oh no!" said Libby, "When did this happen?"

"I had no idea until I got here this evening and found this waiting for me."

Judith showed Libby the letter she'd received. Libby scanned it quickly, and, to her dismay, saw the name of the purchaser, Coleman Properties. Seth's company.

"It says we've only got thirty days before the new owner takes over," Judith continued. "I don't know where I'll be able to run the classes from now. I can't think of any space locally that's big enough and doesn't cost a fortune to rent. I'm worried about the other groups too. A lot of the people who come to the lunch club on Wednesdays are elderly, so they can't travel far to another one."

Libby stayed silent. How long had Seth been planning this? How could he not have warned her?

"It's going to be such a loss to the community," another woman said.

"It won't be the same without the Scouts here. I wonder if another group will have room for them all . . ." commented a man, his greyhound pulling on her lead, reminding him that she was supposed to be here to play with the other dogs.

"I'm sorry," blurted out Libby, suddenly. "I forgot there's . . . something I need to do and I won't be able to stay . . . So silly of me!"

Before anyone could comment, she hurried back out of the hall with a very reluctant Barney tailing behind.

* * *

Libby was home again in fifteen minutes and she let herself in and put Barney in his crate so he couldn't get up to any mischief. She didn't even bother to take off her coat and hat but rushed upstairs to Seth's office, managing to pause for long enough to knock and wait for Seth to reply "Come in" before she entered.

"We'll take a five-minute break," said Seth to his computer screen. He turned his attention to Libby. "What's the matter?" he asked. "I'm in the middle of this meeting . . ."

"You bought the community centre," she blurted out.

"And the land attached to it, yes," replied Seth. "Was that all?"

"Why didn't you tell me?"

"I haven't seen you today."

"You did the whole deal in one day?"

"I left a message for my solicitors about it on Saturday night when we got back from the dog show. They contacted the council this morning with a cash offer which was accepted. There's no need to overcomplicate these things."

"And you're going to destroy the building?"

"The plans are to knock it down and build office buildings, or potentially divide it up, build on some and sell the rest on. I haven't decided yet. I've been looking for the right plot for a while, but it was only when Judith mentioned that the community centre was going to be sold that it clicked what a perfect opportunity it was."

"But what about all the people who use the community centre?"

"There are other centres, Libby. I'm sure they can take their Pilates class somewhere else."

"It's an important part of the community," argued Libby. "All sorts of people rely on it. Did you know my friend puts on a free yoga class there every Wednesday for autistic kids? It means a lot to them."

Seth's stern facade seemed to waiver briefly, but he said, "The deal's been done," with an air of finality in his voice.

"I can't believe you'd do this," said Libby.

"It's just business," Seth said, shrugging. "Anyway, I need to get back to my meeting." He turned back to his computer.

She'd thought Seth was one of the good guys. Yes, he clearly cared about money, but he'd managed to convince her that what he did improved things. Knocking down the much-loved community centre definitely didn't improve anything. And to tell them just before Christmas as well!

Libby went back down to her flat, and, before she could think better of it, she messaged Robert: *Are you free tomorrow evening?*

She only had to wait a minute before a reply pinged back.

Of course. Come here and I'll cook. See you at 6?

Great, Libby replied before throwing her phone on the sofa.

CHAPTER 15

It felt strange to be ringing the doorbell of her old home the following evening. She'd managed to avoid Seth all day, saying she was too busy to join him in taking Barney for a walk at lunchtime. He and Barney had gone off together in the car, and when they returned an hour and a half later, Barney went upstairs to Seth's office. In hindsight, she sort of wished she had spoken to Seth. She hated when they argued. A large part of her felt like turning right around and going home to him. Maybe she could change his mind about buying the community centre. If she caught him when he wasn't working . . .

"Hello," said Robert, opening the door. He leant in to kiss her lips, but Libby subconsciously turned her head a little so he got her cheek instead.

"Hi," Libby said. "I bought some Ben and Jerry's for pudding."

"My favourite," Robert said, smiling. He looked nervous.
"I know."

Libby felt a wave of discomfort. It would be so, so easy to fall back into a life with Robert. A life she'd been perfectly fine with at the time. But now . . . in many ways she was happier now than she had been with Robert, even accounting for the upset of breaking up with him so suddenly. She was certainly more fulfilled in her job now than she'd been in any job before. She felt more valued, and, probably for the first time in her life, like she wasn't constantly being pushed to do more by the people around her.

She followed Robert into the house. It looked empty without all of her things around. She surreptitiously checked the spot on the carpet Barney had peed on and could swear she could see a stain. She bit her bottom lip to stop herself from laughing.

"Would you like a glass of wine or a beer?" Robert offered.

"I'm driving," Libby said, "but I guess I could have one drink."

Robert did a good job of appearing unfazed at the news she wouldn't be staying the night.

"I'm making lamb biriyani, so a beer?"

"Thanks," said Libby. Lamb biriyani was what Robert always cooked for a special occasion or if they'd quarrelled. Robert handed her a drink. "I hope you got naan," she said, sitting on a stool at the kitchen's breakfast bar.

"Of course," Robert said. He seemed to relax a little. *This can't be easy for him*, Libby thought, before reprimanding himself: if it hadn't been for him cheating on her, they wouldn't be so awkward around each other. She would be getting in from a long day at another job she hated, and they'd probably bicker about who was going to cook before resorting to pasta and probably crashing on the sofa to binge a box set. She would likely never have met Seth, or Sarah and Jamie, never got to cuddle Barney and teach him to wait with a treat balanced on his nose (not that he was anywhere close to mastering that anyway) . . .

Libby's phone beeped, "I'd better check that," she said. She unlocked her phone and the WhatsApp message flashed up: *Where are you? Can we talk? Seth*

"Sorry, it's just my boss," Libby said, putting her phone back in her pocket. She didn't know what to reply, and it would be rude to type away on her phone.

"Messaging you at eight o'clock at night?" Robert said, frowning.

Libby really didn't want to go into the intricacies of her relationship with her boss, and she especially didn't want to explain the fact that the message was somewhat personal, so she said, "Yeah, well, I don't always keep regular nine 'til five hours."

"Maybe it should be. What if you move back in with me?"

"Robert, I said I was willing to spend some time with you. I'm not ready to talk about moving in with you, and even if I was, my job is a live-in position. It's written in my contract."

"You can't always be prioritising him. He takes advantage of you."

"I'm perfectly capable of sticking up for myself, thank you," said Libby, her hackles rising.

"You're a glorified dog walker!"

And dog trainer, thought Libby, but she considered it wise to keep that particular fact to herself. In fact, she was sorry she'd even mentioned Barney to him in the first place.

"I love my job, Robert," she said. "It's the first job I've had that seems to fit. And Seth doesn't take advantage. It's just a job that's not as conventional as others. I've begun helping out with some of Seth's charity work, and it means a lot to me."

"You can do so much better."

"I don't want anything better," said Libby firmly. And suddenly it was crystal clear what she needed to do. Seth had listened to her when she'd explained she didn't want to pursue her photography professionally, but Robert wasn't listening to her about this.

"Robert," she said, her tone softening, "I'm glad that I've seen you again so that the last time wasn't you in bed with another woman . . ." Robert opened his mouth to interrupt her, but she put up her hand. "Please let me finish," she said. He stayed silent. "We were together for a long time, but we're over now. I've moved on, and I'm happy. I hope that you can be too."

She got up. "I'm sorry, I think it's best I don't stay for supper."

"There's no need to leave . . ."

"Yes, there is," said Libby, gently.

"Do you not trust me, is that it?" Robert asked.

"That's partly the problem," she admitted. "But I also don't think we're right for each other. Stepping away from us gave me the chance to see that." *And meeting Seth*, she realised. "I'm glad we got to see each other again."

* * *

Libby drove back to Whitehaven with tears in her eyes. She knew beyond a doubt that she'd done the right thing, but that didn't make it any easier. She was still sad.

She opened the front door of the house as quietly as she could, but, of course, Barney heard and came running to greet her. He was closely followed by Seth.

"Where have you been?" Seth said. "I've been messaging you."

"I didn't realise I needed to report my comings and goings to you," snapped Libby.

"Of course, you don't," said Seth. "Sorry. Are you . . . alright? You look like you've been crying."

"I'm fine," said Libby, walking towards the door to her flat. She turned back to face him. "Are you still going through with your plans to destroy the community centre?"

Seth sighed. "Yes, I'm still buying the plot of land, which was being offered for sale, which the community centre is currently on."

"Then I'm handing in my notice," said Libby, firmly.

"You're what?" Seth looked shocked.

"I'm handing in my notice," Libby repeated. "I can't work for someone who would conduct business the way you do. You're destroying something vital to the community."

"The plot is worth a lot of money," Seth said. "It's not being utilised at the moment. Would you really leave over this?"

"You don't need any more money and the community centre is being utilised plenty," Libby replied. "I believe I need to give you two weeks' notice. I'll have it to you in writing tomorrow morning."

"Don't you think that's a little extreme, Libby?"

"No, I don't," Libby replied. "You might not care about the impact your choices have on people, but I do."

She marched into her flat without allowing herself to look back.

* * *

Libby was up early the next morning. She hadn't been able to sleep so she figured she may as well get her resignation letter written. Barney was thrilled to have his friend awake and made her laugh as he ran around the garden chasing his tail.

She showered, made herself a coffee and sat down at her laptop, determined to be positive. She was doing what she needed to do. She lasted about a minute before she put her head in her hands. She couldn't believe she was giving up the only job she'd ever loved. That she was making herself unemployed and homeless. That she was giving up her new friends and, most of all, Barney. She couldn't bear to think about the fact that in just two weeks she might never see him again. But, she told herself firmly, if that was the case then it was what had to be done. She knew Seth would allow her to see Barney if she wanted to, but she needed to make a clean break from her boss.

She should call Anna. Check she was okay. . . But what would she say?

She could still hardly believe that he was going to destroy the community centre. And for what? A load more money? She couldn't work for someone like that, but her resignation was about a lot more than that. She was in love with Seth.

She'd known for a while but hadn't wanted to admit it. Last night though, when she was with Robert, she couldn't deny it to herself any longer. She'd wanted to be with Seth, even though she was furious with him about the community centre. And that thought terrified her.

It had hurt when she'd discovered Robert had cheated on her, but nothing like how it would hurt if it had been Seth. But what hurt more was that she could also never be with him. Even if he had been interested in her as more than his girl Friday, and, yes, perhaps now his friend, he wouldn't want her as his girlfriend. Not Libby, who always seemed to say or do the wrong thing. She'd thought at the Christmas party that she might possibly have been in with a chance, but she'd been kidding herself. He'd just been being kind to her because she didn't know anyone there.

And even if he did like her back . . . how long before it went wrong and then she'd be out of a job and a home anyway? She might as well make a quick break.

She quickly typed out her resignation and emailed it to Seth before she could waste any more time feeling sorry for herself.

She needed to work out where she was going to live and find a new job. She sighed; just before Christmas wasn't the best time to do either. She checked her bank account, which was looking healthier than it had in years — Seth paid well, and as she didn't have to pay for a car, rent or much food, she had a lot left over . . . She'd go on an adventure, she decided. As soon as possible. A proper adventure, like she loved. Something that would give her the time and space to work out what she wanted to do with her life and a chance to heal her broken heart.

CHAPTER 16

The next couple of days went by with Libby becoming more and more miserable at the thought of leaving behind the new life she'd built for herself. She called Anna and her friend had been lovely, reassuring Libby that there was nothing she could do to stop it and even advising her not to quit her job. But Libby knew what she had to do, for her morals as well as her heart.

She kept out of Seth's way as much as possible, and he seemed to be doing the same. They played pass-the-puppy as a very confused Barney got twice as many walks and treats as usual.

She only had to last until the 23 December, she kept repeating to herself. That was when she'd be finishing work for Christmas and heading to her parents' house with as much of her stuff as she could fit in the car. She'd booked off until the 28th when she'd drive back, work her last few days and pack up the rest of her things ready to leave on January 2. Melissa had already said she could store some stuff at her flat while she travelled rather than having to drive it all the way to Somerset.

Libby had decided to drive across America on Route 66, a proper road trip. She'd fly out to the east coast and hire a

149

car. She'd distract herself over Christmas by planning her route and buying the kit she'd need so she wouldn't be stuck focusing on Seth and how much she'd miss him and Barney.

She tried to be excited about her adventure, but she was too sad, and, for the first time she could remember, her wanderlust seemed to be missing. But she determined that it would pass when she was sitting in an American diner with a burger and a road map in front of her, planning where she'd drive the next day.

* * *

During her lunch hour two days before Christmas, Libby was packing, ready to head off to Somerset as soon as she'd finished work for the day. She'd had presents for her parents carefully wrapped and packed for weeks and she'd leave Barney's present for him to have on Christmas Day. She'd already said goodbye to Jamie and Sarah and exchanged little gifts. She'd packed hers from them so she could open them on Christmas morning.

Libby had Michael Bublé playing in an effort to get in the festive mood. She needed to cheer up before she got to her mum and dad's. She didn't want to spoil their Christmas by being miserable. It was bad enough that she'd have to tell them she was going to be looking for yet another job.

Her mum rang, interrupting her organising. "Hey, Mum," she said.

"Hello, darling," her mum said, coughing. "I'm so sorry, but I've got bad news — your dad and I both have the flu."

"Oh no!" said Libby.

"Your dad started coming down with it yesterday and then I work up feeling dreadful this morning. We've been in bed all morning."

"You must be ill — that's not like you at all."

"We don't want you to catch this. It's horrible," her mum explained. "And I don't think I'm going to be up to much, so I think we're going to have to cancel you coming."

"I could come and look after you? Make you soup and things," Libby suggested.

"That's lovely of you, but all we want to do is sleep at the moment, and I'd feel terrible if you got sick and had to miss work when you've only been at your new job a couple of months."

Libby's heart sank. Of course, her mum was right. There was no point in her going and catching whatever horrible lurgy they had, when it didn't sound like her mum and dad would even be up to celebrating.

"Okay, Mum, but if you need me, I can be with you in just a few hours."

"Thank you, darling. Do you think you'll be able to find somewhere to spend Christmas?"

"Don't worry about me, Mum," Libby said, endeavouring to sound as cheerful as she could. "You and Dad get better, and I'll visit you in the new year."

"Alright, darling. I'll give you a call on Christmas Day."

"Speak to you then. Bye!"

Libby slumped down on the sofa feeling completely dejected. She'd been so looking forward to going to her mum and dad's for Christmas. To get away from Seth, and from worrying about getting a new job and a home. She'd longed to be with her family, enjoying all the little Christmas traditions they'd done since she was tiny. She gave in to tears as she allowed herself a few minutes to feel sorry for herself.

There was a sudden knock on her patio doors. Seth and Barney had obviously returned early from their walk.

She got up and went to let them in, furiously wiping away her tears. Barney ran around her legs, and she bent to stroke him.

"Hi— Are you alright? What's happened?" asked Seth, concern written all over his face.

Libby considered saying she was fine, but it was very clear that she wasn't, and she didn't want to lie. "My mum called," she said. "She and my dad both have the flu and so I won't be going home for Christmas."

"Oh no!" said Seth. "Do they need anything?" She could tell he was mentally calculating what he could do to help. But that was Seth all over, always trying to fix everything.

"They say they're alright. I offered to go and look after them, but they just want to sleep."

Seth nodded. "So where will you go for Christmas now? Robert's?" A flicker of distaste passed over his face.

Not wanting to fill him in on yet more misadventures in her romantic life, "Robert's going to his parents, so no, not Robert's."

Seth stood, obviously considering he hadn't had a full answer to his question.

"I don't know," said Libby finally, attempting bravado. "There's my friend, Melissa . . ."

Seth put his hand on her arm. "You could always stay here, and have Christmas with Barney and me," he said. "And my mum, who's coming for lunch on Christmas Day. She'd like it if you were here. I don't know if you've noticed, but I don't exactly go all out for Christmas usually . . . I mean, if you don't get any better offers and if you wanted to."

"Thank you, but . . ."

"It would be awkward?" Seth finished for her.

"Just a bit."

"We're both adults, I'm sure we can put our differences behind us for a few days so that Barney enjoys his first Christmas."

This drew a little smile from Libby.

"Think about it," said Seth. "I'll catch you later."

Seth left and Libby sat back down on the sofa, bringing Barney up onto her lap for a cuddle. She regretted it instantly as he had wet, muddy paws.

Should she stay? What were her other options? She didn't want to impose on people at Christmas, especially if they had family coming. She knew Seth wasn't exactly planning a huge Christmas. He still hadn't put any decorations up.

It would be nice to be with Barney and to give him his presents on Christmas morning, and it wasn't like she and

Seth had to spend every minute together. She could watch a load of Christmas films and ignore Seth's existence most of the time. And he was right, they were both adults, and they were capable of being civil to each other.

Her only other option was to book a last-minute flight somewhere, but for the first time in her life, that idea didn't appeal.

She picked up her phone and messaged Seth: *Okay, a truce for the festive season?*

Meet me in the kitchen at 6 to discuss terms, said the reply.

Libby smiled before scolding herself. She was far too easily charmed by Seth, but she'd just have to endeavour to protect her heart until Christmas was over.

* * *

At 5 p.m., Libby closed down the lid of her laptop. Her Christmas holiday time had officially begun. She had an hour before she was due to meet up with Seth, so she clipped Barney's lead on, grabbed a torch, and set off to take him for a walk on the Hill. She didn't end up needing the torch, the streetlights along the avenues provided enough light she found even though it was completely dark by now. She should be on her way to her mum and dad's now, she thought.

When they got back, Libby unpacked her bags before heading into the kitchen. She was a few minutes early, but Seth was already there, pouring two glasses of red wine. He handed her one.

"A toast," he said, "To our Christmas truce."

"We haven't finalised the terms and conditions yet," Libby pointed out.

"Can I suggest no work talk?"

"I think that's very sensible," nodded Libby. "And we're going to have to do something about this house. I'm not spending Christmas in a house with no Christmas decorations. We can use my little Christmas tree, but we need some tinsel and some fairy lights or something . . ."

"Tinsel, really?"

"Yes. I am not waking up in a house on Christmas Eve with no tinsel."

"Okay, fine," agreed Seth, putting down his glass. "In that case, I'd better go and buy some."

"Where are you going to go? It's quarter past six in the evening!"

"Morrisons," said Seth, firmly. Seeing the incredulous look on Libby's face, he added, "I do know where the supermarket is."

"Alright," said Libby with a shrug.

"I'll be back in a while," said Seth. "Enjoy your wine and think about the rest of your terms and conditions."

Seth left and Libby went back into her flat, closely followed by Barney. She put the tree on a coffee table and stood back to admire it. It looked ridiculous, but it was better than nothing. Then she plugged the speakers into her phone and soon Bing Crosby's 'White Christmas' filled the room.

She looked around . . . she'd done all she could to make the place look and sound Christmassy for the time being, but what she needed to do now was make it smell Christmassy.

* * *

When Seth returned, the house was filled with the scent of baking sugar cookies. He followed the smell into the kitchen. "I never thought I'd see you in an apron," he commented. "I feel like I should take a photo to commemorate this moment."

"Don't you dare!" Libby growled.

"They smell amazing," he said, picking up a golden cookie from the cooling rack. He took a bite. "These are good!"

Libby laughed. "You needn't sound so surprised," she said. "Anyway, what did you get?"

"I've brought one load in. I'll go back out and get the rest now."

Libby followed Seth into the hallway. "This is a lot!"

"Yeah . . ." he admitted. "Just wait until you meet Frosty . . ."

He went back out to the car and returned with a large box with a photo of an inflatable snowman on the front.

"Oh, wow!" Libby exclaimed. "That is going to be awesome!"

Seth looked through to the drawing room. "You moved your tree in there?"

"Yeah, we've got to have a tree, and it's better than nothing."

"Well, I've got another plan. Finish your baking and then get tinselling. I bought up every piece they had. I'll be back soon."

Before she could question Seth, he'd gone back outside again. Libby looked at Barney and shrugged, "Let's get tinselling, dude!"

* * *

Libby had just managed to drape the last piece of tinsel over the drawing room's fireplace when she heard her name being called. She hurried to the back door and opened it. A rather sweaty and pine-needle-covered Seth stood outside. "Give me a hand through the house with this," he grunted, pulling a large Christmas tree into the utility room.

"Oh," said Libby, her face falling. "You cut that down from the garden."

"Yep," said Seth proudly. "Using a saw and everything. What's the matter?"

"It's just that, I'm a bit sad that the tree's dead," Libby admitted.

"Seriously?"

"Yes, it was a beautiful tree!"

"I thought you'd want a real tree, for the smell and everything . . ." Seth sighed and ran his hand over his head. "How about I get Jamie to plant three more trees in its place?" he suggested.

"That would be lovely. Thank you," said Libby, laughing.

"You know you're a complete pain in the bum, don't you?" said Seth.

"I have heard that, yeah."

They ventured out to the tool shed with torches to find something to put the tree in and the next hour was spent wresting it into position. Libby held the tree straight, while Barney supervised, and Seth shoved bricks in the bucket it was standing in to keep it upright.

"Okay . . . let go," said Seth, cautiously.

Libby released the tree and it listed a little to the left. They stood back to examine it.

"It's a bit wonky," said Seth, his head to the side.

"It's perfect," judged Libby. "Let's stop fussing and get some baubles on it."

Libby was pretty sure Seth had also bought up all the baubles the supermarket had. There were boxes and boxes of Christmas tree decorations, and Libby ripped them open eagerly. The tree Seth had chosen was at least eight feet tall and needed a lot to cover it.

Seth set about organising the lights. He'd picked up four sets of white lights and an extension cable, and meticulously wound them around the tree, driving Libby almost mad with frustration at how long it was taking. Finally, the lights were done and they could decorate.

"I got a selection of colours in case you had a theme in mind," Seth explained.

"The theme is Christmas," said Libby, as she added a couple more baubles to a branch.

"Gotcha," muttered Seth, "Be right back."

He returned with wine and handed Libby her glass. He sat down on one of the three large chocolate-brown leather sofas.

"Aren't you going to help?"

"You're doing a great job," said Seth, closing his eyes. "Barney," he called, softly, and the puppy climbed up next to him.

Libby continued decorating the tree but sneaked a peek at the tired pair. Her heart melted at the sight of them cuddled up together. Stop it, she told herself. You're mad at him . . . but she wasn't completely convinced.

"Ta da!" called out Libby as she placed the last cheeky Santa in a sleigh ornament on the tree.

Seth and Barney opened their eyes.

"Let's turn on the lights! You do the honours," Libby offered.

Seth got up and walked over to where the lights were plugged in. "I now declare this tree decorated," he said solemnly before switching the lights on.

"It's beautiful!" exclaimed Libby.

"It's very . . . cheerful," said Seth.

"Thanks! There's nothing for the top though," said Libby.

"There should be a star somewhere," Seth said. "Give me a minute."

He disappeared back out into the hallway and returned with a large, golden glittery star. He climbed up the stepladder he'd brought in so they could reach the higher branches and placed the star on top of the tree.

"Brilliant!" Libby exclaimed.

"Now that we're finally done with the tree, are you hungry?"

"Starving," admitted Libby.

"Fancy a Chinese?"

"Absolutely."

"Cool. Is there anything in particular you want?"

"Surprise me," said Libby.

* * *

Note to self, mused Libby at the sight of the three bags of food that arrived half an hour later, *Seth tends to order basically everything on the menu if you don't tell him exactly what you want to eat.*

"How are we going to get through all this?" she said.

"We can have any leftovers tomorrow," said Seth, opening a carton of barbeque spare ribs.

"Isn't this too greasy for you to eat?" asked Libby, helping herself to a spring roll. "I thought you'd order just like chicken and broccoli or something."

"It's Christmas," said Seth, his mouth full of dumpling.

* * *

There were indeed a lot of leftovers, but not as much as Libby had imagined. Seth could eat a lot when he put his mind to it.

They put the leftover food in the fridge and loaded the dishwasher.

"Thanks for a fun evening," said Libby, smiling. "The place looks great."

"It's certainly . . . brighter," said Seth. She could imagine how deeply offended his whole being was by the tinsel strewn everywhere and the riot of colours that was their Christmas tree.

"I'll see you in the morning then," said Libby.

"See you in the morning."

"Seth," said Libby.

"Yes?"

"It's nice being on a truce with you."

* * *

Libby was woken by Barney at seven the next morning. "Okay, okay," she grumbled as she got up. "I get it, it's your first Christmas Eve, you're excited." She pulled on her dressing gown and trainers and walked through to her sitting room to let him out of the patio doors and into the garden.

She shivered — it was a cold day. Perfect for binge-watching Christmas movies. She wondered if Seth would mind her hanging out in the drawing room so she could watch them on the big screen and look at the Christmas tree. She smiled at the thought of the Christmas tree in all its garish glory.

She showered and dressed in a cosy hoodie and tracksuit bottoms. It was a relaxing day today. She decided not to bother with make-up, since the only person she was likely to see was Seth, but he would likely be locked in his study all day working, she imagined. Maybe they'd have dinner together tonight . . . she could cook for him to say thank you for last night.

Libby went through to the kitchen with Barney and got herself some granola for breakfast. She glared at the coffee machine, wishing she worked out how to use the stupid thing. There was no sign of Seth, but then he was so tidy, he could have held an early breakfast buffet for twenty and it would all be cleaned up by now.

She was loading her dirty bowl and spoon into the dishwasher when she heard the front door opening. Barney ran into the hallway.

"Hi!" Seth called out, "I'll be through in a minute! Careful, Barney, I don't want to step on your paw by mistake."

Seth joined Libby a couple of minutes later.

"Where have you been?" Libby asked.

"I needed to pick up something for my mum," Seth answered. "What are your plans for the day?"

"I hadn't really made any," said Libby.

"Good," said Seth. "I've got some work I need to do for a few hours. But then we're going for a walk with Barney. There's a nature reserve nearby I've been wanting to explore."

Libby looked out of the window, "But the weather's disgusting," she argued.

"It's supposed to dry up a bit later, and imagine how devastated Barney will be if he doesn't get a walk . . ."

"You could take him by yourself," Libby suggested.

"Barney will be disappointed not to have us both there," argued Seth. "Why are you trying to spoil his first Christmas?"

Libby laughed. "Okay, fine."

"I'll see you at lunchtime then," said Seth.

"Sure. Do you mind if I use the television in the sitting room? I want to watch a Christmas movie and look at the Christmas tree."

"Of course, I don't! This is your home," said Seth. Then he looked embarrassed. Worried he'd mention that Libby was only going to be around for just over a week, she quickly said, "Thanks!" and went into the sitting room to choose a film.

"Why do you have Disney Plus?" she called through to Seth. "Are you a *Frozen* fan?"

"*Star Wars* geek," he shouted back.

Hmmm, thought Libby, she would not have guessed that.

She beamed when she saw *The Muppets Christmas Carol* available to stream. She went back into her flat to get her favourite blanket and then got settled on the sofa opposite the television, with Barney snuggled up next to her.

"Do you want a coffee?" Seth yelled from the kitchen.

"Yes, please!"

Seth brought her through an americano a moment later, "*Muppets Christmas Carol*, eh?"

"Got a problem with that, Coleman?" Libby asked. It felt good to be using his nickname again.

He smiled and Libby could have kicked herself for how good that made her feel.

"Not at all," replied Seth. "It's a favourite of mine. Mind if I join you?" He indicated to the sofa Libby was on.

"Oh, no, of course I don't mind," said Libby, wiggling over to give him some more space. Barney gave a little grumble at having his pillow moved.

Seth sat down and stretched out his legs with a little sigh that sent shivers down Libby's spine. Did he have to sit so close to her?

The sofa was large and, even with Barney on there with them, there was plenty of room, but Libby still felt very close to Seth. She realised she was holding her breath and let it out in a burst.

"Are you alright?" Seth asked.

"Absolutely," Libby replied.

She tried to concentrate on the film and felt she was doing a pretty good job until she heard Seth humming.

"Are you humming along with Kermit?" she asked.

"Bob Cratchit, technically," commented Seth.

"I thought you had work to do."

"I lied," Seth said. "I didn't want you to feel crowded so I was trying to leave you alone."

"What happened to that idea, then?"

He grinned. "You put on my favourite Christmas movie."

They sat in companionable silence. Libby even managed to start to relax a little.

"Are you finally going to get some work done now?" Libby asked Seth as the credits rolled.

"No," said Seth. "I've decided that I'm officially on my Christmas holidays. As I can't remember taking a Christmas holiday since I was at university, this is a big deal for me."

"Exciting!" said Libby. "And what are you going to do on this holiday?"

"I'm going to start by getting you to help me blow up Frosty so he can go outside, in pride of place by the front door."

Libby proceeded to hold Frosty as upright as she could while Seth pumped him up using the foot pump provided. Twenty minutes later, a rather wonky snowman was solemnly sitting outside.

"Very welcoming," declared Libby.

"I agree," said Seth.

"Of course!" said Libby. "By the way, are you going to cook tomorrow?"

"Yeah, but I usually get food delivered from a restaurant at Christmas." Seeing the look of horror on Libby's face, he added, "Don't panic! We're not doing that this year, but I've never cooked a Christmas dinner before so I may need some help."

"Neither have I," she admitted, "but I'm pretty sure we can figure it out together."

"I've got a food shop arriving at six this evening. Hopefully, I've remembered everything."

"We'll manage if you haven't," Libby assured him.

Libby's phone beeped with a message from Melissa: *How's your Christmas Eve going?*

"It's my friend," Libby said. "The one who owns the agency you went through to find me. I hadn't told her yet about not going to my parents. I'd better give her a call."

"See you later, then," said Seth, "I'll take Barney with me."

Libby went into her flat, sat down on her sofa and called her friend.

"Merry Christmas Eve," she said when Melissa answered the phone.

"Hello! Merry Christmas Eve to you too. How are things?"

"Good," said Libby, "but not exactly as I'd planned. Mum and Dad are sick so I'm staying in Weybridge with Seth . . ."

"Oh no! Why didn't you call me?"

"It's fine, really . . ."

"You can come here for Christmas! There must be something going around because my family are sick too. I'm off to a party tonight, you can come too, and then we can veg tomorrow."

"That's sweet of you," Libby said, "but, honestly, I'm fine here. Seth and I have called a truce for Christmas and we're having a good time. We've got a tree and everything."

"Sounds very cosy . . ."

"It's just for Christmas," said Libby.

"Well, are you positive you don't want to come round tomorrow?"

"Thanks, Mel. I've said I'll help Seth cook for his mum so I'd better stay here."

"Are you sure he's not taking advantage of you?" she insisted.

"No, not at all, he's being really . . . lovely actually."

"Libby, it was only a few days ago that you were leaving your job and were going to be homeless in a couple of weeks."

"I still will be. I'm just ignoring those things over Christmas."

Melissa laughed. "Sounds very healthy."

"I'm fine really. Seth's not a terrible person; he's just not someone I can work for."

"Alright, but I'm here if you need me, okay?"

"Thanks, and Merry Christmas! I'll speak to you soon."

Libby wandered back out into the main kitchen to get a cup of tea, glancing out of the window to see Seth outside, playing with Barney in the garden. It didn't seem to be a very complicated game, as far as she could tell. It seemed to involve Seth chasing Barney and then Barney chasing Seth. Sometimes Barney added a ball into the mix.

Libby watched them for a minute until Seth turned and caught her. He waved. Embarrassed at being caught peeping, Libby slunk away from the window and filled the kettle.

Just as the kettle had boiled, Seth came in bringing a wave of cold, Christmassy air. "Chinese leftovers for lunch?" he suggested.

"Sure," said Libby.

"And then we'll head out for our walk."

"You're still set on that then?"

"Yep," replied Seth, "And we need to be out of here by half one."

"Any reason why?"

"It gets dark early," said Seth, shrugging. "Do you really want to be walking around a nature reserve at night?"

"Not really," admitted Libby.

"How was Melissa?" Seth asked.

"She was fine. Her family's also ill though."

"Does she want to join us for dinner tomorrow?" Seth suggested. "There should be plenty of food for one more."

"Um . . . I don't know. I guess I could invite her."

"I'm picking my mum up at midday. I can get her as well if she wants, and drop her home in the evening."

"That's nice of you," she said, hesitantly. "Are you sure?"

"Yes."

"Alright, I'll message her," Libby said.

They ate the leftover Chinese food and then got ready to go out. It had been lightly snowing all day and wasn't showing any sign of stopping yet. Libby wrapped herself up in waterproofs and wellington boots.

Her phone dinged with a reply from Melissa:

Do I want to spend Christmas Day in the swanky house and meet the crazy millionaire? Sure I do! What should I bring? Don't worry about him picking me up though, I'll bring my car.

Libby smiled. This was turning into a very unusual Christmas.

"Hurry up!" Seth called from the hallway.

"Okay, okay!" she replied, hurrying through. "I don't think a few minutes is going to make a huge difference!"

She caught the corners of Seth's mouth twitching at the sight of her waterproofs. "Expecting to swim, are you?"

"At least I'll be fairly warm and dry," she retorted, trying not to smile in response.

"Come on!" said Seth, hustling her towards the door. "Let's go!"

* * *

They walked until it was almost dark and then went to a dog friendly cafe for coffees and Barney's first puppacino. They drove back onto the Hill at quarter to six, waving at the security guard in his hut as they went past. They were all tired and very muddy, especially Barney.

"We'd better give Barney a bath when we get in," said Libby.

"Yeah, we could shower him in your bathroom."

"Why would we cover my bathroom in mud and dog hair?" replied Libby, indignantly.

"It's the closest one to the door," explained Seth, driving through the gates to Whitehaven and along the drive.

"He's your dog, he should use your—" Libby stopped talking and gasped. The house was covered in white Christmas lights. They were around the windows and door, around the eaves of the roof . . . not even the garage had been excluded. "It's beautiful," she said.

"I hoped you'd like it," said Seth.

Libby was almost speechless. "How?"

"A company came to do it. They were arriving at 2 p.m. That's why we needed to leave when we did."

Libby laughed. "I wondered why you were even crazier about being on time than usual."

Seth's phone rang as they were getting Barney out of the car. "It's Sarah," he said. "You answer it. I'll wash Barney."

He waved to Frosty and took the puppy inside. Libby accepted the call as she followed them into the house, "Hi Sarah, it's Libby," she said, closing the front door behind her.

"Oh, hi Libby! What are you doing with Seth? I thought you were going to your family for Christmas?"

"It's a long story!" Libby said. "Is everything alright?"

"Yes," replied Sarah, "Except my stupid oven has decided to break on Christmas Eve! It's only Ethan and me, thankfully, but I won't be able to cook our Christmas lunch. I was calling to ask Seth if I could come and use his kitchen to cook it tonight so I could just heat it in the microwave tomorrow."

"I'm sure he wouldn't mind, but I've got a better idea," said Libby.

* * *

Seth came downstairs a quarter of an hour later with a much cleaner Barney. "He got me so soaked, I had to have a complete change of clothes myself," he grumbled. "How was Sarah?"

"Her oven's broken, so I invited her and her son tomorrow. I hope that's alright," she added, suddenly worried she'd overstepped a line.

"Of course, that's fine," he said, breezily. She inwardly sighed with relief.

The gate buzzer went. "That's the food delivery," Seth said. "I hope we've got enough for everyone now. The shops will all be closed."

"Don't worry about that," Libby said. "Sarah's bringing her food to add to it. Her meat's already defrosted so it would only be wasted if she didn't cook it tomorrow anyway."

"Brilliant. Could you open the door to the delivery driver and get them to put the food in the kitchen? I'll be back in a minute."

"Sure."

By the time Seth returned, Libby had unpacked most of the shopping. "I think you thought of everything," she said.

"We've got two more guests for tomorrow," Seth said. "I called Jamie and he and his girlfriend are coming over as well. I think they were both sort of dreading attempting to cook the turkey crown they'd bought. We'll just chuck it in the oven with everything else."

"This is going to be crazy!" Libby said.

"It's definitely not how I thought my Christmas was going to be."

"You're telling me."

"Okay," said Seth, getting into action mode. "You pour wine and put away the rest of the food. Oh, why don't you open some of those pistachios?"

"And what are you going to do?" Libby asked, her hands on her hips.

"I am going to cook you a delicious dinner which we can enjoy before moving into the sitting room with the popcorn and sweets you see before you, and watching another Christmas film. I would like to suggest *Home Alone*."

"Fine . . ." agreed Libby. "But I want to watch *It's a Wonderful Life*. I always watch it with my mum on Christmas Eve."

"Agreed. I'm blaming you if I don't like *It's a Wonderful Life* though."

"You've never seen it? It's brilliant!"

"I'm withholding judgement. Hurry up with those snacks, would you?"

CHAPTER 17

Libby woke up on Christmas morning with a smile on her face. She'd had a brilliant Christmas Eve. She still couldn't believe the lights on the house. And the dinner Seth made had tasted amazing. And she was sure she'd seen Seth wipe away a tear at the end of *It's a Wonderful Life*.

Barney spotted she was awake and gave a little woof to remind her he was there. Libby got up and let Barney out of his crate. "Merry Christmas, Barney!" she said. She kissed him. "Let's get you some breakfast and then you can have your presents."

Her phone dinged with a message from Seth: *Are you up?*

Barely, Libby replied.

—I have coffee . . .

—I'm in my pyjamas!

—The ones with hearts on? I'm in my pyjamas too. I want to give Barney his presents.

Seth wasn't going to give in. She could smell the coffee as soon as she stepped into the hallway and followed her nose to the kitchen.

"You *are* in your pyjamas!" she said when she saw Seth. How did he manage to still look so muscular?

"Of course," he replied. "It's Christmas. You've got to open your presents in your pyjamas."

Libby had put her presents for Barney under the tree before going to bed the night before, along with the presents she'd been given from Sarah, Jamie and Melissa and a little something she'd got for Seth a while ago before she'd quit her job.

There were extra presents under the tree now from Seth to Barney.

It was then that she noticed three stockings, stuffed to overflowing, hanging from the mantelpiece.

"When did you have time to do those?" she exclaimed, taking down her stocking, before remembering that, really, the puppy should go first.

"I have no idea what you're talking about," said Seth. "I'm as surprised as you are that I've been good enough to get anything but coal again this year."

Libby laughed and unwrapped a big chew stick for Barney. She gave it to him, hoping it would keep him busy enough for her to open her stocking presents.

"This is amazing," she said, popping a large chocolate coin in her mouth. "I still can't believe you did this."

Seth bit the head off a chocolate Santa. "Like I say, no idea what you're talking about. Now, come on, Barney, let's open your big present."

Libby's stocking was filled with foodie treats from the posh delicatessen in the town.

Seth pulled a large box out from under the tree and helped the very excited puppy to open it. Inside was the most comfortable-looking dog bed Libby had ever seen. She was very tempted to curl up in it. "This is so you can be comfy when you're helping me in my office," explained Seth, as he ruffled the puppy's ears. He was rewarded with a lick.

Barney also received a new water bowl with his name engraved, two new food bowls, a new harness, and lots of squeaky toys and treats.

"Do you think we've spoilt him?" Libby said.

"Of course not," said Seth, indignantly. "It's no more than the best puppy in the world deserves."

There was another large present tucked behind the tree. Libby knelt down and pulled it out assuming it was yet another gift for Barney, but the label read, '*To Libby, Happy Christmas, from Seth.*'

"This one's for me," she said, surprised.

"You'd better open it then," Seth replied.

Libby tore off the wrapping paper to reveal a backpack. Puzzled, she took it out and quickly realised it was a camera backpack — a Gomatic waterproof one — the kind of bag she'd dreamt of having to keep her equipment safe.

"It's a camera rucksack, for when you're travelling," Seth explained.

"Oh wow," said Libby. It was also top of the range. "How did you know which one to get?" she asked. She couldn't keep the smile from her face.

"I noticed which camera you use," replied Seth with a shrug which didn't come across as quite as nonchalant as he was perhaps going for.

"This is great! Well, thank you so much. I got you something too, but it's only small." She handed him the little package.

"I saw them online and couldn't resist," she explained.

Seth burst out laughing as he unwrapped a pair of socks with Barney's face printed on them. "These are absolutely brilliant," he said, putting them on straight away. "Thank you."

Libby then warmed up some pastries in the oven for breakfast while Seth tidied up the wrapping paper and made them more coffee.

"You've got forty-five minutes tops to get yourself ready," Seth declared as Libby put the last bite of a pain au chocolat into her mouth. "We need to get cooking."

"Have you checked how long our turkey crown takes to cook?" Libby asked.

"A couple of hours or so," Seth said. "I figured we'd get everyone's meat sorted when they get here."

"See you in forty-five then, Coleman," said Libby, giving a salute before marching out of the room.

"A maximum of forty-five minutes!" Seth called after her.

* * *

Libby showered and put on a long-sleeved red dress she'd bought specially for Christmas a few weeks ago and blow-dried her hair and did her make-up. "And with four minutes to spare, eh, Barney?" she said, as she checked herself in her wardrobe mirror.

When she rejoined Seth in the kitchen, she wasn't surprised to see him in his usual daily uniform. "Not dressing up for Christmas, then?"

"I'll put a party hat on later for you. I hope we have enough crackers . . ." He looked at her. "You look lovely by the way."

"Thank you," Libby replied, turning her face so Seth couldn't see her blushing.

"Have you spoken to Robert to wish him a Merry Christmas?" Seth asked, appearing deeply absorbed in checking Barney's new collar fitted correctly.

"Not very subtle, Coleman."

"Well, have you?"

"No. I broke up with him again, not that there was really anything to break up, but . . . anyway . . ." Libby watched Seth for his reaction.

He stood up and said, "I would comment, but it's none of my business, so I'll keep my mouth shut."

"I appreciate that," said Libby.

They looked at each other and then both burst out laughing.

"I'm going to make some mince pies," said Seth. "We'll have to decide the full menu once everyone's here with all the food, and we'll just eat when it's done."

170

"I can start prepping some veg," Libby offered. "And then we can do the rest when we have it. This is bonkers," she added.

* * *

Seth left to get his mum and Libby took Barney for a walk on the Hill. There was quite a little community of dogwalkers out to wish Merry Christmas to.

She opened the gates to Melissa soon after getting back.

"I'm so glad you could come!" she said, hugging her friend once she was out of her car.

"Are you kidding me? I would not have missed this," said Melissa. "Whose idea was the snowman?"

"His name's Frosty and he was Seth's idea," Libby said.

"I brought orange juice and bubbles to make mimosas," said Melissa, handing two full carrier bags to Libby.

"Perfect!" said Libby. "Let's get inside before Barney breaks down the door to get to you."

Seth returned with his mum, who'd brought homemade Christmas puddings with her, and Sarah and her son, Ethan, with everything for a Christmas dinner for two. Last were Jamie and his girlfriend, Amy, who was shy and sweet, also with the food they'd been planning to cook.

Melissa made everyone drinks while Seth and Libby sorted out the food. Ethan was helping Seth's mum, Ann set up the new phone Seth had got her, and Jamie and Amy were in the garden with Barney.

"The good news is, I don't think anyone will starve," said Seth. "The bad news is that we're going to need to make about fifteen side dishes . . ."

"Let's sort the meat out first," Sarah suggested, reaching for her apron behind the pantry door.

"Don't you dare!" said Libby and Seth added, "Absolutely not! You are not cooking today!" He handed her a mimosa. "We'll open presents as soon as we've got the turkey in the oven,

171

and then you can give Ethan a hand setting up a Nintendo Switch he may find under the tree."

"You spoil him," Sarah said, hugging Seth.

"No more than he deserves," said Seth. "And I'm looking forward to thrashing him at *Mario Kart* later."

* * *

It was 11 p.m. before Seth and Jamie finally admitted defeat against Ethan and Amy on the Switch, and everyone got up to leave. Libby watched Seth and Ethan fist bump. Seth, it seemed, was very good with teenagers.

"Are you all sure you don't want anything else to eat or drink before you head off?" Seth asked.

"Please, no!" said Sarah. "I never realised you were such a feeder."

Everyone else confirmed they were full to bursting.

Melissa had offered to take Ann home, and Jamie and Amy would drive Sarah and Ethan so that Seth was able to enjoy some wine with his Christmas dinner. Ethan had encouraged this as he'd hoped the alcohol would dull Seth's reflexes when gaming.

Seth and Libby waved everyone goodbye, and Seth offered to take Barney out for a last little walk on the Hill.

Most of the cleaning up had been done throughout the day, but there was still stuff left from the impromptu supper of cheese, pâté, crackers, grapes and mince pies they'd managed to force down at nine. Everyone had been too keen to return to the video and card games they'd been playing to worry about tidying up properly.

Libby emptied the dishwasher and began loading it up again. She was just wiping down the island when Seth and Barney returned.

"That was a brilliant Christmas Day," said Libby.

"The carrots were a little overdone and could have done with a smidge more honey—"

"Seth, it was *brilliant*," repeated Libby, instinctively touching his arm. Seth turned his head and his eyes met hers. Suddenly, Libby's stomach flipped as neither of them broke eye contact. He looked at her like he was drinking her in.

"Oh," said Libby, moving closer almost without noticing. He liked her, she realised. He liked her a lot.

"Yeah, oh," said Seth. He tentatively reached out his hand and ran it down her cheek, never breaking eye contact.

"Please, don't make me resist anymore," he whispered.

They leant forward simultaneously, smiling at one another, at the secret they'd uncovered, and kissed.

CHAPTER 18

Libby sneaked out of bed the next morning, leaving Seth asleep. She quietly pulled on some jeans and a hoodie and went to let Barney — who'd been firmly relegated to her office overnight — out of his crate, before putting on her trainers and coat and taking him outside. She needed a few minutes to herself to process what on earth had happened between her and her soon-to-be ex-employer.

It was certainly a turn-up for the books. It turns out she and Seth were a very good match, at least in one way anyway. Obviously, this changed things hugely between them and she wasn't sure how that left them now. She wanted to be able to go over things more, but it was absolutely freezing and starting to snow, so she and Barney headed back inside.

"Hey, you," said a very sleepy-sounding Seth as she attempted to sneak back into her room.

"Hi," Libby replied. He looked delicious, all warm and crumpled, and softer than his usual self.

"What are you doing up?" Seth murmured.

"It's relatively late for Barney," Libby said. "And for you, come to think of it."

"It's nice here," said Seth. "Come back and join me."

"I should really . . ."

"It's Boxing Day," Seth said. "There's nothing for you to do."

"I'm just not sure it's such a good idea . . ."

"Christmas truce, remember," said Seth, holding up the edge of the duvet.

"Do you think we should talk about . . . this and whether it's sensible?"

"I can think of other things I'd rather do," said Seth. "And Christmas isn't the time to be sensible."

"You're always sensible."

"I'm turning over a new leaf. Don't overthink this, Libby."

Libby sighed, took off her clothes, and climbed back in. "I would like it recorded that I said this was a bad idea."

"And I'd like it recorded that you need a better mattress," said Seth, pulling her to him.

* * *

Seth made them both scrambled eggs and smoked salmon bagels for breakfast.

"I was thinking of going for a swim," said Seth.

"I knew you wouldn't be able to resist the lure of exercise for long," teased Libby as she got up and loads the dirty plates into the dishwasher.

"Well, I wouldn't say I've been entirely sedentary," said Seth, his lips brushing the back of her neck.

"Can I join you?" Libby asked.

"Sure, but you'll probably just do a few laps and then lie on a lounger and pretend to read while ogling me," Seth replied.

"As if!" said Libby, flicking him with a tea towel.

It turned out Seth was half right. Libby didn't end up doing much swimming, but she did a lot more than just ogling him from afar.

* * *

"I'm going to have to go out for a couple of hours after lunch," Seth said, as they got out of the pool. "I promised I'd take Ethan out shopping for some new trainers in the sales. Apparently, his mum doesn't know the cool shops to go to."

"That's so nice of you," said Libby.

"I like spending time with him," Seth replied, "He's a cool kid."

* * *

Libby took Barney for a walk while Seth was gone. The sun was shining and she didn't want to miss it. And, as daft as she realised she was being, she wanted something to do while Seth was out. She'd miss him if she stayed in the house.

She made her bed and tidied her flat, then put Barney's harness on him and got him in the car. She drove for about twenty minutes to a little woodland she'd heard of with a walk that shouldn't be too long for Barney's still developing legs. It was cold, but the weak winter sun felt good on her face and being out in the fresh air helped to clear her mind.

When she was with Seth, it was like all she could think of was him. She needed to consider any of the repercussions of what they were doing, she told herself firmly. But then, actually, what were the repercussions? She was leaving her job so it wasn't like he'd fire her once he got bored of her, although she couldn't imagine Seth doing that anyway. And there was no one else who would be hurt by their actions. Just her. Was she prepared to accept that? What she wasn't prepared to do, she realised, was stop because she'd be hurt in a few days when it ended. She was having the most incredible Christmas. As she couldn't turn back the clock and change the fact that they'd slept together, she might as well enjoy the ride for the short time it lasted, and not think about how broken her heart would be at New Years.

* * *

"What do you want to do now?" Libby asked once they'd finished cleaning up after the supper of Christmas leftovers.

"I've got another Christmas tradition that needs reviving from my childhood," Seth said. "I always used to watch a *Star Wars* film on Boxing Day with my uncle."

"Seriously?"

"I'm afraid so, but I'm not above bribing you with hot chocolate."

"Fine!"

"Have you seen *Star Wars* before? Like, any of the films?"

"No," admitted Libby, "But I'll give one a try for you . . . and the hot chocolate."

Seth began heating the milk and lit the fire in the sitting room. Libby fetched blankets from her flat and got comfortable on the sofa, and Seth brought the drinks and the last of the sugar cookies she'd made.

"I need to get myself some . . . blankets and things," Seth said. "Cushions, you know, the sort of stuff you have."

"Yes, you do," Libby agreed. "I really love that tree," she said with a contented sigh.

"Good," Seth replied, settling in next to her. For the time being at least, Barney chose to curl up by the fire.

"This is definitely not how I imagined spending my Boxing Day," said Libby, as Seth put his arm around her.

"Me neither," Seth said, kissing her gently, "But I kind of like it."

* * *

"Do you have any interest in going out anywhere today at all?" Seth asked the next morning.

"Honestly," Libby replied, "if it wasn't for Barney, I would happily spend the rest of the day in bed with you. Why? Did you want to do something?"

"Nope," said Seth, lazily tracing circles on her stomach.

"Can we watch some more *Star Wars*?"

"I knew you'd like it!" said Seth. "I'm sure we can fit that in."

"Do you want to go and see your mum?"

"She's gone to visit her cousin in Yorkshire," Seth said. "She won't be back until the new year."

By which time I'll be gone, thought Libby, sad at the thought that she'd never get to see Seth's lovely mum again.

"Hey. Are you alright?" asked Seth, noticing the change in her expression.

"Absolutely," said Libby, forcing a smile on her face. "But hungry. Let's get some breakfast."

* * *

The next few days flew by in a blur of happiness, and it was only when Seth asked her what she wanted to do that night that she realised it was New Year's Eve.

"Of course, New Year's. I've lost track of the days." The truth was that she purposefully hadn't allowed herself to think about the dates and to count how many days she and Seth had left. She was trying to enjoy every moment while it lasted.

"There's a party I've been invited to, or we could invite some people round here . . ."

Libby pulled a face.

"Or we could just be the two of us?" he suggested.

"Technically three of us," said Libby.

"How could I have forgotten about you, Barney, eh?" Seth said, reaching down to give the dog a stroke. "What would you like to do? You want to drink champagne? And probably not even bother about staying up until midnight and go to bed early instead?"

Libby laughed. "I'll have to call my mum and dad at midnight at least. Mum would be upset if I didn't."

"Fair enough, we can stay up until midnight if you must, but I'm not promising you'll remain fully clothed," Seth said, kissing Libby on the mouth.

She stroked his face, smiling. "That sounds like a very good compromise to me," she said.

She was happy but it was as though they were both dancing around, neither wanting to admit the significance of them seeing in the New Year together, Libby thought.

"How are your parents now?" Seth asked. "Still improving?"

"Yeah, they're a lot better now. Planning to redo Christmas one weekend in a few weeks."

"Maybe I could come with you," suggested Seth, hesitantly. "Try to make a better impression on them than I did the last time they saw me."

Libby froze. This was against the rules of the Christmas truce. They didn't talk about what happened with 'them' after this bubble they were currently in burst.

"Seth," said Libby, putting her hand on his arm. "I gave in my notice. I'm not going to be here in a few weeks. I'm not even going to be in the country."

"But," said Seth, "I thought, after the last few days . . ." Libby's heart clenched. She'd never seen Seth look so vulnerable. She wavered. Did he think they could be together long term? That this wasn't a fling?

"It's just a run-down community centre," Seth said. "The people who use it can easily find somewhere else. Would you honestly make yourself jobless again and go back to temp work because I want to make a profit from it?"

Oh, he didn't want the inconvenience of finding another girl Friday. Had it finally dawned on him that not everyone would be willing to put up with his crazy whims?

"It's important to the community, and you don't need that profit," Libby said, hurt that a stupid business deal obviously still meant more to him than she did. And angry with herself for believing that might no longer be the case.

"That's not quite how business works," said Seth. "If I don't keep making a profit, how am I supposed to continue paying my staff and funding my charity?"

"There must be plenty of other plots you could buy."

"Libby, you do realise, that if I didn't buy that centre, someone else would. It was being put up for sale anyway."

"That's not the point!"

"Of course it is!" snapped Seth and he walked out of the room.

CHAPTER 19

Libby repacked her bags the next morning. What a terrible start to the new year. Her eyes were red and sore from all the crying she'd done the night before, but there was no point in crying any more. It wouldn't help anything.

She didn't want to leave her job, or Barney, or Seth, even though she was mad at him, but she didn't have a choice. Seth's love was his business, not her, and it seemed he still didn't care who he hurt as long as he made money.

Melissa had immediately offered to let her stay for as long as she needed as soon as Libby had called and explained what had happened. She'd go there today, and then to her parents when they were fully better and give herself a chance to take stock of her life. She'd cancelled her plane ticket. She'd just be running away from her problems and she knew it wouldn't help. It would also mean she'd have even less money to see her through until she found herself a new job.

She didn't know how much of her stuff to take. She couldn't fit everything in the boot anyway so she'd have to leave some of it. Plus it would take her time to pack, and the way she felt, she just wanted to get as far away from possible from Seth. How stupid she'd been to think she could just sleep with him and there would be no repercussions . . . If she was honest with herself, she'd known there would be repercussions, she'd just been too stupid to realise how bad they would be. If she'd thought it hurt not having Seth before, it was a thousand times worse now.

She was wasting time being maudlin. Giving herself a mental shake, she carried her bags through to the hallway and took a look around, trying to take in everything she could of what had been her home. She realised how much more she felt for this house than for the one she'd shared with Robert, not because of the size or the grandeur of Whitehaven, but because of its inhabitants.

Oh, how she would miss this beautiful house and the people in it. She'd thought she'd finally found a job she loved and she was happy in. Would she be so lucky again? At least now she knew what it was like to go to work and enjoy it. She promised herself she wouldn't be taking on any more temp jobs. She knew she needed a job that was a little unusual and wasn't the same day to day. Something with a charity would be nice. But she'd think about that in a little while. Once her heart had had a chance to heal.

Barney woofed from the top of the stairs where he'd been upstairs with Seth. He came galloping down the stairs to join her and she scooped him up. He was getting so big, she wouldn't be able to do that for much longer. She received a lick on her cheek and she laughed. Barney may be a traitor but he was a very cute one.

The Christmas tree in the living room caught her eye, and she went in to take a last look at it. It would most likely be down by the time she came back to pick up the rest of her things. She smiled as she remembered how proud Seth had been when he'd dragged it in and set it up. It was still kind of wonky, but she liked it like that.

There was an A4 envelope on the floor with her name on it which definitely hadn't been there the night before. Libby put Barney down and opened it to find a thick wad of paper inside. It was a contract. She scanned the front page quickly, trying to work out what it meant.

"A belated Christmas present," said Seth from behind her.

She turned to face him, her heart thumping.

"Does this say what I think it does?" Libby asked.

"Yes. I haven't been able to get it formally drawn up yet, but I'm gifting the community centre to the town. The roof is being fixed next week as well. I still think that spot is prime for development, but . . ."

"But what?"

"I don't need the money and you're right: the community centre is important to people. The only proviso I'm asking is that a youth club is run there a couple of nights a week, but my charity will finance that."

"Seth, this is . . . amazing," Libby finally managed to say.

"It's the right thing to do," said Seth. "But I'm doing it for you."

Libby's heart leapt. "For me?" she said.

"Of course," said Seth, simply. "Haven't you noticed that you always tend to get your own way with me? I don't know how you manage it, but it's what happens."

"But I thought you were so set on this," said Libby.

"I was. But you were right about what you said. I don't need that land, but . . . I've built my business from nothing and it's been my life for so long, I know I can be too focused on it. When I was two, my dad left me and my mum. Just disappeared, leaving us with nothing. My mum worked cleaning the houses on this hill because the people living here paid more, and then she came home to our one-bedroomed council flat and slept on the sofa so I could have the only bed.

"Sometimes I came to work with her during the holidays and I promised myself that one day I would live in one of these houses. I never went without, thanks to her, but I wanted more. I wanted better. So I worked hard at school and university and started my company with the money I'd saved, since I got my first part-time job when I was fourteen. As soon as I was able to, I bought my mum her house. I wanted to buy her one on this hill, but she didn't want that."

He shook his head.

"I saw my dad again for the first time a few days after the first interview I did, when people began to be interested in my success. He turned up asking for a handout, and, like an idiot, I gave it to him. I hear from him every six months or so, always wanting more money. Normally he writes but he's shown up before, at my office. But there was something about seeing him with you that day which sent me over the edge."

"You were pretty scary," said Libby, gently. "I'm so sorry you had to go through all that."

"Don't feel sorry for me. My mum was amazing. I'm just trying to understand why I'm the way I am. Once my mum had everything she needed, I turned my attention to trying to help teenagers who are struggling, as I did. That's why I set up my charity, and to do that, I needed my business to be successful. I've always stuck to my guns and prided myself on never allowing myself to be influenced by anything unrelated when I'm making business decisions. And that's served me well. But then you came along, and I found myself at puppy-training classes, drinking watered-down mulled wine out of a plastic cup, chopping down trees, and . . . trying to think up ways to spend more time with you." Seth didn't meet her eyes. "I couldn't help but try to make you happy, but the only thing I swore I wouldn't be swayed in were my business decisions, and I thought that would be fine, but then the community centre happened. I couldn't bear to upset you, but I was also too proud to give in."

"Thank you," said Libby quietly. "Everyone at the centre is going to be so pleased, and the youth club is a brilliant idea."

Seth took a deep breath. "Libby," he said. "Please don't go. I want you to stay. Even if you don't want to work for me anymore. At least until you find somewhere else to live. You could just keep looking after Barney until you find a new job."

"I can't, Seth," said Libby.

"Why not? There's no need for us to argue anymore. The community centre is safe," Seth said. "Barney is going to miss you so much."

"I know he is," said Libby, "And I'm going to miss him too, and . . . everything here, but . . ."

"But, what?" said Seth, taking her hands in his. "Tell me. I'll make it better. Anything. Just don't leave like this."

"My leaving isn't only about the community centre. I can't stay because I'm in love with you," said Libby, pulling her hands away. "I know it's stupid, I'm completely wrong for you. Why would someone like you ever want to be with a flake like me? But I can't help it, and I'm not going to get over you if I stay here."

"Libby, can't you see you're perfect for me?" said Seth, gently. "You balance me. You stop me from being the idiot I so often am. You're what makes me happy, even more than having a dog." He threw an apologetic look at Barney.

"But that goes against what those studies say," whispered Libby, allowing her eyes to meet his.

Seth grinned. "Who would have believed it? And as for you being a flake, Libby, you're the most reliable, trustworthy person I know. So why would you want to get over me?" asked Seth. "It makes things much simpler if you're in love with me as well. I thought I was going to have to work so hard to win you over. I was planning months of gentle wooing."

"Wait a second. What did you say?" said Libby, hardly daring to believe it.

"I'm in love with you, too, Libby. I have been for quite a while. Why do you think I've been acting so crazy? Cancelling my dance classes because I don't want to dance with anyone else but you; turning up at your ex's house because I was worried about him trying to surprise you there; cutting down trees in my garden by myself . . . You know I got into a lot of trouble with Jamie for that."

"How long, exactly?" Libby said.

"Probably since I saw you stomp out of my pool house," said Seth, a smile forming on his lips.

"That is quite a while," teased Libby.

"So, it hasn't been so long for you?"

"Well . . ." Libby said, "there was something about you rushing to rescue Barney from drowning at about that time . . . but it does make everything much more convenient if you're in love with me as well."

"Quite the time saver, really," muttered Seth, gently pulling her towards him.

"Really very convenient," Libby replied, leaning in to kiss him.

"So, you'll stay?" asked Seth, before adding, "As my girlfriend?" His mouth was an inch away from hers.

"I'll stay," confirmed Libby. "As your girlfriend, but also your girl Friday. Please," and Seth finally let her have her kiss.

THE END

THE JOFFE BOOKS STORY

We began in 2014 when Jasper agreed to publish his mum's much-rejected romance novel and it became a bestseller.

Since then we've grown into the largest independent publisher in the UK. We're extremely proud to publish some of the very best writers in the world, including Joy Ellis, Faith Martin, Caro Ramsay, Helen Forrester, Simon Brett and Robert Goddard. Everyone at Joffe Books loves reading and we never forget that it all begins with the magic of an author telling a story.

We are proud to publish talented first-time authors, as well as established writers whose books we love introducing to a new generation of readers.

We have been shortlisted for Independent Publisher of the Year at the British Book Awards three times, in 2020, 2021 and 2022, and for the Diversity and Inclusivity Award at the Independent Publishing Awards in 2022.

We built this company with your help, and we love to hear from you, so please email us about absolutely anything bookish at: feedback@joffebooks.com.

If you want to receive free books every Friday and hear about all our new releases, join our mailing list: www.joffebooks.com/contact

And when you tell your friends about us, just remember: it's pronounced Joffe as in coffee or toffee!

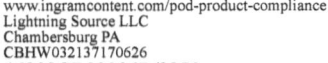